BLOOD MARKED

A SELBY JENSEN PARANORMAL MYSTERY

JULIETTE HARPER

PROLOGUE

The high-pitched keening rose to a deafening pitch. The man beside me moaned in terror, "Oh, God. It's happening again." Before I could respond, shock waves rippled across the room. The sharp staccato rhythm of hooves on the hardwood floor signaled the coming attack.

The force of the impact caught my client full in the chest, throwing him against the wall with bone-crunching force. He slid down, scrambled to his hands and knees, and spider-crawled away.

"Do something!" he wailed. "He's going to kill me."

"Probably because you killed *him*, you dumb shit," I said, fumbling in my pocket for the vial of Holy Water I'd picked up from Father Peyton's office. My go-to exorcist picked a hell of a time to visit Rome.

I deal with the supernatural for a living, but casting demons out in the name of Our Lord and Savior is not among my qualifications. The assistant at the church gave me the appropriate ritual text, but he didn't provide any suggestions about juggling the book, the Holy Water, and a 9mm pistol.

The answer probably involved faith and putting down the gun; neither of which struck me as viable options.

"Come on!" I taunted. "You think you're so bad. Show yourself."

Across the room a burst of sulfur smoke erupted leaving a horned goat facing me. "He has to die for what he did. Do not stand in my way, human."

"Look," I said. "I'm willing to live and let live. If you don't want your hosts to get turned into barbecue, don't inhabit farm animals. Look what happened to Legion and that herd of pigs."

At that, the goat lowered its head and charged. Screw this shit. My gun was loaded with Holy Water hollow points — that was sacramental enough for me. I took a split-second aim at that patch of hair between the animal's horns and pulled the trigger.

The bullet hit the target about five feet in front of me. The apparition exploded, emitting a black wraith-like demon that roared with anger. Now that I had the damn thing out of the goat manifestation, I uncorked the bottle of Holy Water and threw it.

"I cast you out, unclean spirit."

A blinding light filled the room. The windows burst open. In an instant all the air was gone, and then I heard a bird singing in a tree outside.

For a wild second I had the urge to steal a line from *Poltergeist* and say with a bad accent, "This house is clean."

Instead, I glared at my blubbering client and said, "My fee just doubled."

"Anything," he sobbed. "Anything. I'll never eat meat again."

Yeah. Hi. My name is Selby Jensen. I'm not your average private investigator and the vampire who sent me on this job was going to get a major goddamn piece of my mind when I got home.

1

When Thaddeus stretched his legs, the denim covering his boots retracted, revealing gaudy yellow cactus flowers stitched into the leather uppers.

Dex Jensen studied the sharply pointed toes and high, slanted riding heels of the vintage Western footwear. "How do you walk in those things?"

"Son," Thaddeus said, staring at the boots with loving admiration, "these are custom made. Bought'em at M.L. Leddy's in San Angelo in 1922. Finest bootmaker to be had in West Texas. Back in that life, I didn't just walk in these boots, I waltzed clean across the state in every dance hall I could find."

Resisting the urge to roll his eyes, Dex said, "Knock it off, Thad. I recognize a stolen song lyric when I hear one. Besides, weren't you already here when Ernest Tubb recorded *Waltz Across Texas*?"

The older man's bushy salt-and-pepper eyebrows shot up with indignation. "Hold your horses. I didn't *steal* that lyric, I *wrote* it. Where do you think Ernest Tubb's nephew, Billy, got the idea for that song? We had a drink in Fort Worth in 1964. Next thing I know, my song's on the radio and Billy's claiming credit."

Dex frowned. "I thought you made the trip in '28?"

"Yep, August 14, 1928, in Amarillo," Thaddeus said. "Drew me a bull no man could ride."

This time Dex did roll his eyes. "For starters, you're too old to still have been riding bulls in 1928. Second, that's a line from a Garth Brooks song called *Beaches of Cheyenne.*"

"You caught me," Thad admitted. "Radio waves travel real nice across the void. Marconi got me all set up to pull in the stuff I enjoy, but sometimes I surf the decades. I like that boy Garth. He's a rounder. Listening to good country music helps me forget how I did make the trip."

"What happened to you?"

"It was a bull, but not one I was riding. I let the son of a bitch get me up in a corner. Ran a horn through my chest and tossed me like a ragdoll. I lay out there in the pasture bleeding to death and gasping for breath until the lights went out. Hell of a way to make an exit. Even now when everything's good again, I think about it."

Dex didn't answer. He let his mind drift to a dirty, abandoned warehouse where he was supposed to meet an informant. Instead, he heard heavy breathing in the shadows and reached for his gun — too late.

A blast of rank animal breath assaulted his senses as sharp teeth ripped the flesh at his neck. The wet, tearing sound registered in his brain before the pain hit his nervous system. Blood rushed into his windpipe and filled his lungs, coming back up in a crimson spatter when he coughed.

The gore sprayed across the werewolf's face filling the animal's eyes with pleasure as it reared back chewing on an obscene white tube Dex realized had been ripped from his throat. By then his vision had begun to dim; blessedly he didn't feel the rest of what the hulking beast did to his body.

Instead, Dex drifted in a hazy mist for what seemed like hours before he stared down at the mangled remains of his own body. His first conscious thought as an earth-bound ghost had been the agonized realization of what his death would do to his wife.

Beside him on the porch, Thad said, "Try not to relive it, son. That was only one way your story came out. You're more than that now."

"I know," Dex said, scrubbing at his face, "but you're right; the memories don't go away. Selby and I are still dealing with the fallout of what happened in that warehouse, but let's get back to the problem at hand."

"I'd like to tell you that I have an answer for that, Dexter, but I don't. You should know by now that it's a bad idea to make a promise to a woman you can't keep."

Wincing at the use of his formal name, Dex said, "Selby does not do well when she thinks she's being kept in the dark. I don't see why I can't tell her the truth."

"You could tell her," Thaddeus said, "but the question is, would she believe you? She's more comfortable thinking of you as a ghost. The idea fits her belief system."

"That's part of the problem," Dex said. "Selby's understanding of the world doesn't include ghosts who can assume a physical form. The other day she wanted to know if I was an angel."

The old man broke into a cackling laugh and slapped his knee. "That's a good one. What did you tell her?"

"I told her no," Dex said, "but you can understand how she came to that conclusion. I did show up in the wake of the Blessed Mother."

Thaddeus nodded. "It's hard for folks to understand that people in pain call out to the expression of comfort and goodness most likely to answer them in their hour of need."

"The angel thing was a big leap for Selby," Dex said. "Faith is not her long suit in life. She's lost too many people."

"That's why she likes to spend time with the middle grounders," Thaddeus said. "She figures somebody who's already dead won't leave her again."

The two men sat silently on the covered porch looking down a grassy slope toward a quietly flowing river.

Struggling to keep his voice steady, Dex finally said, "If I could tell her the truth, it would give her more hope for the future, but where she is now, she has to continue doing her chosen work. I went back because she couldn't get over my absence. I saw the potential alternate course she was headed down. I couldn't let her take that dark path."

"You made a choice; she made a choice," Thad said kindly. "In some place, that darkness may overtake her yet."

"It may," Dex agreed, "but all I can do is work with my perceptual path. I chose to go back in part to keep her from allowing pain and grief to overwhelm the good she can do before her next phase."

Thaddeus stood up and stretched, stepping toward an ancient ice chest sitting against the wall of the clapboard house.

"All the choices are valid, son, you know that. You want an orange pop?"

The non sequitur made Dex laugh. "I haven't had an orange pop since I was ten years old."

"Then you're overdue," Thaddeus said. He lifted the lid of the chest and extracted a pair of tall bottles, prying the caps off with an old-fashioned wall-mounted opener.

Accepting the drink, Dex tilted the bottle back and let the neon liquid flow down his throat.

"Man," he said, "that takes me right back to the fat stock show when I was little. Grandpappy always bought me an orange pop and a sack of roasted cashews as soon as we got to the fairgrounds."

Thaddeus snapped his fingers and produced a red-and-white striped bag. "Like these?"

"Just like those," Dex said, holding his hand out as the other man shook a mound of warm cashews into his palm.

Chewing appreciatively, Dex studied his companion. "What influenced your choice to move back and forth?"

"There's a lot about that world I like," Thaddeus said. "Once I understood that control is an illusion, it was easy to set myself free to explore. I like knowing there are options and that some part of me follows every one of them."

Shifting in his chair, Dex said, "I think Selby would like the part about the options, but it would be hard for her to accept the rest. The passage sounds like a bunch of made up, New Age bullshit until you've lived it."

Thaddeus tossed the last of the cashews from the bag into his mouth, crumpled the paper, and sent it flying toward the galvanized bucket under the bottle opener. At the last minute, he altered the course of the projectile with a flick of his finger to ensure it hit the bucket's rim and bounced inside.

"That's cheating," Dex observed mildly.

"You see cheating, I see the perfect rim shot. All a matter of perception," Thaddeus said. "Look, Dexter, you know your wife better than I do, but from what I've seen, Selby has to make some perceptual shifts of her own before she's ready to embrace the bigger picture. For starters, that woman has to figure out that not all enemies can be defeated at the business end of a Colt."

"Glock," Dex said absently. "Selby prefers a Glock."

"Not the point I was aiming to make."

"Sorry," he said. "Look, I'm not trying to be difficult here.

Selby does the work she's meant to do. I have to be careful not to throw her off her journey."

Thaddeus pushed his battered Stetson back, reaching under the crown to scratch his head. "Yes, you do," he said. "It all makes sense on our side of things, but on hers, not so much. You wanted my advice, so I'm gonna give it to you. Keep on letting her think you're a ghost, and that being near the Blessed Mother magnified your energy."

"There's just one problem with that, Thad," Dex said, "how does she know it wasn't the Shadow Man who 'magnified' my energy?"

The old man regarded him with thoughtful eyes. "Reckon that's where the faith part has to kick in. You've got a strong soul, Dexter, and a real depth of purpose. I've never known anyone to embrace duality the way you have. If anybody can convince Selby, it's you."

Emptying the last of his soda, Dex stood to leave. "Same time next week?" he asked.

"There you go again thinking chronologically," Thad grinned. "Whenever you show up, I'll be sitting right here."

Dex stepped off the porch and stretched in the bright sunlight. "*Here* is an awful pretty place."

"So's *there*," Thaddeus said, putting his head back and pulling his hat low over his eyes. "You only see the world you make."

Dex started toward the river but turned back when the old man called to him. "Before you go, there's a gal named Olivia Reynolds you need to know about. She's gonna be crossing paths with you all real soon. Her world view is getting expanded at the moment. Poor kid is gonna need some help."

"Good expansion or bad?"

"Pointy toothed kind," Thaddeus replied. "Selby will take it on because she's good with the bloodsuckers, but look for the curveball, Dexter. It's headed your way."

2

"That might be the cleanest gun in the state of Texas."

I ignored the statement, keeping my attention on the parts of a Glock Model 19 on the table in front of me. A protective layer of newspapers covered the work surface. My eyes idly played over a headline in the morning paper. "Northside Woman Claims Mass Chupacabra Attack."

Mexican goat killer, my ass. The last six rounds down the Glock's barrel had been directed at the pack of coyotes responsible for that story — and hadn't that been a hell of a lot of fun.

Picture this. The night before, I roll up on a woman in a floral housecoat brandishing a flip-flop (known in these parts as a chancla) at a pack of snarling, mangy coyotes.

There isn't a Mexican kid alive who doesn't fear the Wrath of the Chancla hurled or brandished by their mother, grandmother, or Tia Lupita for a perceived infraction of social or religious etiquette.

The Northside coyotes, which the woman insisted represented the el chupacabra legions of hell, hadn't gotten the Chancla Memo. Typically, coyotes are shy of humans, but this incident involved an attempted rescue of a chihuahua named Eloy who didn't escape the Grim Coyote Reapers.

Chancla Lady was bent on revenge. I guess I should be glad she wasn't armed with anything more substantial than a glorified house shoe. Shoving her aside, I took out the coyotes and then had to deal with the San Antonio police because I discharged a firearm in a residential neighborhood.

I'm beyond licensed to carry, but I'd been up half the night dealing with the fallout, filling out reports about the incident, and participating in Eloy's funeral.

Fast forward 24 hours and I'm looking for some "us" time with my husband. But when we came upstairs to our apartment, Dex didn't take off his leather jacket, which meant he intended to head out again. My disappointment immediately turned to anger, an emotion I tried to dissipate by keeping my hands busy.

Two clips of ammunition lay on the table next to me. One was loaded with seventeen silver bullets. The other held custom Holy Water hollow points made by a gunsmith named Luther who operates a seedy shop a few blocks over.

"You're going out tonight," I said in a flat voice.

It wasn't a question.

Dex leaned against the kitchen counter, arms crossed over his chest. "Yes," he said, "and for the record, I'm not looking to get slugged in the jaw when I come home."

He was referring to an incident a few weeks earlier when I woke up in an empty bed.

My husband has a new habit I don't like. He disappears for hours at a time. I have zero need or desire for the two of us to be attached at the hip. Before he died, we always led our own lives.

Sometimes he worked nights; sometimes I did — but we always met in the middle. We didn't disappear on each other without a word.

The first time I woke up and discovered Dex wasn't in bed with me, I almost lost my mind.

I am not some crazy, possessive bitch. I just got the man back after he'd been dead for five years. Not make-believe dead as in witness protection or dropping off the grid. Honest to God *dead,* dead.

When I reached for him that night and felt nothing but empty mattress, heart-pounding panic surged through my veins.

Had I dreamed his resurrection? Did I really have my man back or had the whole thing been a tequila-inspired dream?

Given how much Patrón I'd consumed in Dex's absence, option number two was entirely possible.

If there's an elegant way to deal with grief, I've never found it. From the moment I walked away from Dex's grave, I shut down my feelings, and buried myself in hard work, hard liquor, and hard living.

"Home" was a place to clean my guns and sleep off the benders. More often than not, I crashed on a cot in my office.

No man walking could ever replace the one I put in the ground, but I indulged in the occasional placeholder. Drunken anonymous nights in hotels one grade above sleazy only because I paid the bill.

Those one-night stands meant nothing. I'd face the dawn, hungover and mildly disgusted with myself, vowing I'd never get that low again — until the next time.

If I had known that Dex was always there, watching, and looking out for me, those nights would never have happened at all. But in those days, I couldn't connect with him in whatever passes for an afterlife, and he didn't reach out to me.

Working and chasing the worm kept me putting one foot in front of the other.

That's nothing but urban slang by the way. Real tequila

doesn't have a worm in the bottom of the bottle. Trust me. I drink the good stuff.

Just like I own the best weapons.

Just like I married the best man.

So, given all that, maybe you can sympathize with what I did when Dex strolled into the apartment at six in the morning after his first disappearing act.

It never crossed my mind he'd been out chasing skirts, but I slugged him anyway.

Okay, I kissed him hard and fast. *Then* I slugged him with a right to the jaw so substantial I rocked him back on his heels.

I may not be all that big, but I know how to throw a punch.

Dex stood there, working at his jaw until the joint popped loud enough for me to cringe. I wasn't aiming for permanent damage. I wanted the man's attention. I got it.

"What the hell was that for?" he asked, sounding perplexed.

"I've got a better question for you," I snapped. "Where the hell have you been?"

He didn't give me anything close to a satisfactory answer. I came away from our most recent case, a murder at a girls school with an uneasy awareness that I was now married to a ghost. At least I *think* he's a ghost.

The man showed up in the basement at the exact moment the aura of the Virgin Mary herself faded from the room. That scenario can even cause someone as spiritually ambivalent as me to add two and two together and come up with something bigger than four. I started to suspect my husband might be hiding a pair of wings somewhere.

That first night at the school, I didn't question why I could touch him. The next few days, I didn't question why he popped in at odd moments the way all ghosts do, but then my husband started to get more and more solid.

I assumed Dex worked for the Big Guy upstairs and started

to throw a lot of questions at him. War, crime, poverty, hunger, incurable disease . . . cellulite. What the hell was up with any of that stuff?

(I said I had a list, I didn't say it was prioritized.)

Dex laughed at the angel suggestion, but he didn't give me a decent alternative explanation. All he said was that sometimes he'd have to be gone for a few hours. He asked me if I could accept that.

Still flush with the exhilaration of his return, I said the romantic thing. "As long as you keep coming home, I can accept anything."

Now we're several weeks farther down the road, with several more disappearing acts under our belts, and I'm not so starry-eyed. But before we get to my marital issues, I have to come clean with you about the thing I didn't say to Dex that night that I should have said.

I didn't tell him that when I woke up in a panic with my heart thudding wildly against my rib cage, I went into the bathroom and splashed cold water on my face. I looked into the mirror and saw something I hadn't seen since I was a teenager — my eyes, glowing a soft violet.

That's why I slugged Dex. I hadn't had one of those goddamned episodes in at least 20 years, and I was not about to start having to deal with that shit all over again.

Unfortunately, that wasn't an isolated incident. The night before this tale begins, Dex and I went to bed together. At 3 a.m. I came awake alone, gun in hand, aiming blindly into darkness no bullet can pierce.

My gun hand was steady as a rock, but the rest of me was trembling and terrified. In my dream, my husband hadn't come home. It had all been one of the Shadow Man's twisted illusions.

I sat there, every nerve in my body on high alert, my lungs fighting for air until a pale form materialized beside me.

Helen has been my best friend for as long as I can remember. She died in a car crash when we were 25 — that was fourteen years ago. But unlike everyone else in my life, she came back. Technically, I guess you could call her presence a "haunting" — the standard kind that I understand.

"It was just another dream, babe," she said softly, moving as if to take the gun from me only to sigh when her hand passed through the barrel. "Breathe, Selby. I told you not to eat those enchiladas at 9 o'clock at night."

That got her a laugh, but it came out sounding like a choked sob. I lowered the weapon.

"Should we talk about your eyes?" Helen asked.

"No," I said. "We should not."

Which didn't slow Helen's roll one bit.

"How long has it been back?" she asked.

"A few weeks," I admitted sourly. "Since the first night Dex pulled one of these disappearing acts."

"How have you been dealing with it?"

"Meditating like Maria taught me."

"You have to tell Dex."

"No, I don't," I said, "and neither do you. He didn't even know me when all that crap went down."

"*He* didn't know you, but *I* did," Helen said. "You're going to need help to get it under control again."

"Sixteen-year-old me needed help," I said. "Thirty-eight-year-old me does not."

Wisely deciding to let the touchy subject go for now, Helen said, "Thirty-eight and a half."

I launched a pillow in her direction, which, of course, went right through her. She faded back out of sight, and I went into the bathroom, studying my eyes in the mirror.

A pale violet ring surrounded the irises, but it was fading quickly. I stood there breathing deeply until the abnormal coloration was gone and then I let out with a long, elegant string of cuss words.

Nobody, not even Dex, gets to make me feel that vulnerable. I will be damned if I'm going to have to relive a problem I put to rest 20 years ago. *Hell* no.

At first light, cloaked in the armor of anger, I headed to Luther's for a session with the only therapist I trust: my gun.

3

Embalming fluid. Olivia Reynolds shouldn't have been able to detect the pungent chemical odor, but it permeated the funeral director's black suit and radiated from his pores. The artificial scent mingled with the cloying aroma of casket spray roses with such nauseating power, Olivia thought she might throw up.

Breathing through her mouth to lessen the fetid impact, she whispered, "I'm so sorry. I didn't know there was a service in progress. I'm looking for the caretaker's office."

The somber man pointed down a side hall with practiced gravity. "Third door on the left."

Nodding her thanks, Olivia walked toward the office, grateful for the thick carpet that muted the sound of her footsteps. She tapped lightly on the door and entered when a voice said, "Come on in."

Inside the small, cluttered room a man in work clothes sat behind a desk piled high with papers. "Good morning," he said cheerfully. "What can I do for you?"

"Good morning," she replied. "My name is Olivia Reynolds. I

believe my grandparents are buried in this cemetery. Could you help me find their plot?"

"Sure," he said, wheeling round and tapping on the keyboard of an ancient computer. "Names?"

"Gallo," she said. "Norman and Madeline."

She watched as the man scrolled through the records while organ music from the chapel swelled in the background.

Earnestly, tenderly, Jesus is calling, calling, "Oh sinner, come home."

The last words sent a shiver through Olivia's body as another voice rose in her mind — the voice from her dreams.

We know you're there, Olivia. Come home! Come home!

Olivia snapped out of her reverie when the caretaker cleared his throat.

"Sorry," she apologized. "What did you say?"

He regarded her with kind sympathy. "Were you close to your grandparents?"

Olivia blinked. "Uh, yes, when I was young. I wasn't living near them when they died."

She felt an immediate wave of guilt for lying, but the truth was none of this stranger's business — even if she had known what truth to share.

The man nodded with understanding. "That must have been hard for you," he said, standing and pushing the rolling chair back. "Why don't you follow me in your car, so you can stay as long as you like at their graves?"

Murmuring her thanks, Olivia followed the man out a side door to avoid mingling with the mourners now pouring out of the chapel. He coaxed an ancient pickup to life and gestured at her to follow.

They circled around the back of the chapel and made their way through carefully manicured plots toward the older, more neglected back corner of the cemetery.

When the truck stopped, Olivia parked and got out.

"They should be here," the caretaker said, studying a folded map in his hand. His eyes tracked over the line of headstones and stopped.

"There," he pointed.

Olivia stared at the bare patch of ground. "Where?" she asked.

"There," the man repeated, "between those headstones."

Two feet of struggling grass covered the area separating the granite blocks.

Perplexed, and mildly annoyed, Olivia reached under her dark glasses and rubbed her tired eyes. She didn't have the energy or the patience to follow this guy all over the graveyard until he located the correct plot.

"This can't be the right place," she said. "There's no marker."

"There's no mistake," he assured her. "Your grandparents are buried in a single unmarked grave."

A gust of wind swept over the plot making the map in his hands flap wildly.

Olivia waited until he'd tamed the paper before saying, "Why on earth would that be the case?"

Looking slightly uncomfortable, he said, "It's not an uncommon practice for people who can't afford to buy a full plot."

"But no *headstone*?" she protested.

"Markers are expensive, too," he said. "If there's nothing else I can do to help you, I should be getting back to the office."

"No, I'm good," Olivia said. "Thank you for your time."

She waited until the sound of the truck's engine disappeared to step closer to the grave.

As Olivia stared down, a shadow passed rapidly over the grass. Ducking on reflex, she narrowly missed being struck by a large hawk. Air rushing from the bird's wings swept over her face as distant words pierced her mind.

Let the dead rest.

When the hawk landed in a nearby tree, Olivia met its sharp, intelligent gaze. "What if the dead won't let *me* rest?" she demanded.

Ignoring the bird's penetrating stare, Olivia removed a folding knife from her bag and knelt where she imagined a gravestone would have sat. Sinking the blade into the grass, she cut a square of turf and pried it free with her fingers.

The roots came away with surprising ease, revealing dank, pungent earth. Using the knife as a probe, Olivia searched until the tip made contact with something solid.

Scooping out handful of dirt, Olivia struggled until she pulled a flat metal box free. When she brushed away the clods clinging to the lid, she saw signs of rust, but no holes. The latch, however, refused to budge.

With no other tool on hand, Olivia worked the blade under the frozen hasp and twisted. The hinge broke, but the knife slipped, arcing over her fingers and slicing the flesh. When the lid fell back, drops of blood splattered the scarred leather cover of the book lying inside.

As the crimson splotches began to sizzle, Olivia recoiled from the stench of hot iron. Swearing under her breath, she reached for the volume only to stop with fascinated revulsion.

The crimson flow of her blood reversed course. As she watched, it re-entered her body, slipping through tightening skin until nothing remained but dry, pink lines.

In her mind, the hawk spoke again. *"Hurry. You are not alone."*

Olivia nervously glanced at the surrounding graves but saw no one. Wasting no time, she re-buried the box and tamped the turf in place. Rising to leave, Olivia stuffed the book in her bag only to feel the hairs on the back of her neck rise.

That's when she saw him. A figure in the shadows at the treeline, hands shoved into the pockets of a light jacket. He was grinning.

Sick fear shot through Olivia. She stumbled, caught herself against the car door, fumbled with the handle, and almost fell into the driver's seat.

The man didn't move — he did laugh.

With shaking fingers, Olivia turned the key in the ignition, put the car in reverse, and fled the cemetery.

A 9 MILLIMETER automatic should lean into the hollow of your hand with such intimacy it feels like ballistic foreplay. A perfectly balanced handgun whispers against your skin.

"I'm here for you, baby. You're safe. You got this."

People fail you. They leave. They die. They make you doubt yourself.

But a well-oiled piece? That's a friend for life.

You may fail. *You* may die. *You* may doubt.

A gun does what it was designed to do. You can count on it.

I know what you're thinking. This bitch has an unnatural attachment to her firearms. Damn straight I do.

Your average gun owner? Maybe they take out a rattlesnake with the poor taste to crawl in the wife's flowerbed. Or, at the extreme end, stop some asshole trying to boost the family F150 pickup truck.

My adversaries come with bigger agendas, and hardier constitutions. I carry two extra clips on my belt: one for the aforementioned Holy Water hollow points, and the other (you guessed it) for silver bullets.

There's a reason why my gun needs to be a natural extension of my hand. It keeps me from turning tail and running like some prissy little girl when the fur, and the fangs, come out.

I operate in a world where monsters are real. My job is to keep people like you from finding out that world exists.

But since you're here, I'll let you in on a trade secret. Being well armed is a critical accessory for badassery.

When one of our cases shakes me up, I make a compensatory improvement to my personal arsenal. Call it a coping mechanism.

Coming off the Shadow Man case at the Good News Educational and Salvation Academy, I ordered custom molded grips for my everyday carry.

If you and I are going to keep company even for narrative purposes, you need to understand I'm not the kind of woman who takes comfort in a new handbag or a killer pair of shoes.

The only part of that statement that works for me is "killer."

So there. I'm out of the closet. I'm in a committed relationship with my handgun.

Luther solidified my plan to get in some therapeutic time on the pistol range by calling me the morning after Dex's most recent disappearing act, to tell me the grips were ready. I grabbed a morning gallon of coffee and headed over.

As usual he tried to talk me into a laser sight, and as usual, I told him to go to hell.

I'm not some house cat looking to chase a red dot. When I draw a bead, I know exactly where that bullet will wind up.

Luther and I traded good-natured insults while he switched out the grips, and then I bought a couple hundred rounds of wadcutters and headed for the shooting range in his basement.

Nobody ever gets good enough to skip time on the firing line, but that's not the only reason I like to murder paper targets. Cutting down silhouettes curbs my urge to unload on the living.

I prefer my friends dead for a reason. First, they won't die on me again, and second, they're not nearly as goddamned annoying as the breathers with vital signs.

Anyone peeking into my life that summer morning would have seen a woman who should have been on top of the world. In addition to getting rid of Central Texas' biggest paranormal pedophile, the Powers That Be in the Universe gave me back my husband.

How did that work? Damned if I know.

Five years ago, a rogue werewolf with enough power to shift on the dark of the moon ripped Dex to pieces. We buried him real pretty with all his buddies on the San Antonio police department lined up in their dress blues.

Nobody saw what happened during the "private" interment when I chained the casket in silver to make sure what was left of Dex didn't get furry on the next full moon and claw his way back to the surface.

Don't get it in your head that I'm the forgiving sort. During the next 1,825 days, I lived for one thing and one thing only: finding the werewolf who killed my husband, so I could make him die a slow death, one silver bullet at a time.

Even with Dex back, I still want a chunk of that murdering mongrel. Dex refuses to discuss the topic. He wants me to let the whole thing go. Trust me; I haven't.

That wolf plunged me into hell for five years. God only knows who else he's consigned to those same black depths. But that's a hunt for another day.

So, there I was, not giving much of a damn about anything but revenge, and then a girl named Emily Montrose got her head bashed in at a born-again girl's school. After that, a lot of things happened all at once.

I acquired a friend with a pulse named Ruth Beauchene, a

Cajun witch flying under the radar as the school's headmistress. Now she works with us.

My business partner, a 200-year-old French vampire named Johnny Devereaux, who used to have the hots for me, has fallen head over heels for her.

When Ruth left the school, Ernest, a wildfire elemental, came along for the ride. He'd been getting his kicks impersonating a demon at the academy, but our experiences with the Shadow Man put an end to Ernest's ambitions to earn points with the Dark Side.

Ernest might be a talking ashtray with an attitude, but he's not in league with Satan. As much as he hates to admit it, he's never even met the guy.

Anyway, back to the big event. The night of our final confrontation with the Shadow Man, the Virgin Mary came to the site where Emily Montrose was killed and carried the souls of all the children who died at the school to a better place.

She left one soul behind: Dex.

When the Blessed Mother's aura faded, there he stood. Rugged, handsome, sexy. I fell into him like what I was — a woman dying of thirst. He died a cop and came back as . . . something else.

Trust me, Dex has corporeality, but from what I can tell he still occupies some place between the land of the living and the other side. He's not like any ghost I've ever met.

I still love the man, but I don't understand him anymore. We both changed during those five years. Grief and loneliness whetted the edge of my worldview into a straight razor. I lived on a steady diet of grim determination. No one would ever get close enough to hurt me again.

It made me feel better to believe that Dex never kept secrets from me before he died. Now, we're feeling our way around the truths we need to share but can't speak.

I'm sorry if that disappoints your romantic notions of what our reunion should have been — and was, for the first couple of weeks. Now? We're the definition of "it's complicated."

4

The new grips felt good against my hand. I stared down the pistol barrel and squeezed the trigger. Using the recoil to bounce the sights back on target, I slammed one slug on top of the other over and over again. The icy concentration made me feel safe and in charge.

With ear plugs firmly in place, I didn't so much hear someone join me on the range as feel a presence in the basement. I stepped back from the firing line to see a lean man in jeans and biker boots put his gear down on the long shelf running along the back wall.

Yeah, I'm human. I took in the black hair that curled at the collar of his leather jacket, the drooping moustache, and the laugh lines in his tanned face; I liked what I saw. Blue eyes met mine and the guy gave me a slow, lazy grin. Before I thought, I grinned back.

New Guy laid a Colt 1911 on the padded surface, a solid choice in an automatic, but then he took out something that made my mouth water. A long-barreled Colt Single Action Army, the .45 caliber revolver known as the Peacemaker.

At first, I thought he had one of the re-issues, but then I saw the patina of age and loving care. Damn. An original.

There are six lanes on Luther's range. New Guy could have chosen any one of the remaining five, but he sauntered in my direction and chose the lane to my immediate right.

Even with hearing protection, the roar of the old Colt reached my ears. God, she sounded sexy. Authoritative. Solid. Secure in her reputation as one of the most popular handguns ever made.

She and New Guy had a good relationship. He popped off six shots with studied ease in a pattern so tight I could have laid a quarter over the holes.

When he stepped back I mouthed, "She's a beauty."

He opened the cylinder, dumped the spent cartridges in his hand, and held the gun out to me.

No way in hell I was going to pass up an offer like that. Holstering my Glock, I accepted the Colt, reloaded it from the box on the bench, and took aim. The revolver was heavier than my automatic, but I liked the weight.

I won't lie. She kicked like a son of a bitch but came right back in line. I caught on to the rhythm of cocking and firing and produced a commendable pattern. Not as tight as New Guy's, but deadly enough.

When I handed the gun back, I slipped one ear plug free. "Thanks, man. That's one hell of a gun."

"You're one hell of a shot," he said, offering me his hand. "Hunt Walker."

The words came out in a basso grumble.

"Selby Jensen," I said, shaking his hand. "I haven't seen you in here before."

"Just hit town," Walker replied. "I heard Luther's the man to see for custom work."

Since Luther's best known "custom" work involves supernatural ammo, it was a fair bet Walker and I shared the same profession.

"In town for work or pleasure?" I asked.

That easy grin came back, deepening the lines on his face in a way that had me reminding myself I'm a married woman.

"If you do what you love," he drawled, "you'll never work a day in your life."

In other words, none of your damn business lady.

"Fair enough," I said. "Good shooting."

"Same to you, Selby," he replied. "Maybe I'll see you around."

"Maybe so."

When I went upstairs I poked my head in Luther's work room and said, "What's up with the new guy downstairs?"

"Damned if I know," Luther said, running a cleaning rod through the barrels of a sawed-off 12-gauge. "Walked in off the street and paid for an hour. That's all I know. Why?"

"Oh, nothing," I replied. "He's down there with a Peacemaker popping off patterns the size of quarters."

Luther's eyes lit up. "A *real* Peacemaker?"

"Real as they get," I said, heading out for the walk home. "Catch you later."

Behind me I heard the door of the shop close. I glanced behind me in time to see Luther flip the "Open" sign to "Back in a Few."

I chuckled under my breath. He couldn't resist the pull of that old Colt either. 'Cause I totally noticed the gun before I took a good look at the man holding it.

You can't see it, but I'm giving you my best innocent eyes.

As I walked, I thought about my visceral reaction to Hunt Walker. With Dex back from the grave, I shouldn't have been noticing other men, no matter how good looking or how well armed.

Warning bells went off in my head. I'll cop to being a poor communicator, but when I'm with someone, I don't cheat. That shit does not fly in my book.

No matter how put out I might have been with Dex in that moment, I felt guilty for taking a second look at a complete stranger. Dex and I had to get our act together before we blew the mother of all second chances.

He wasn't going to like it, but Dex was going to have to talk to me. The half-dead man of mystery thing wasn't working for me. My husband needed to know that, before a real wedge formed between us.

In the interest of full disclosure and scene setting, I'll admit I hadn't been in the greatest mood even before Dex's latest nocturnal disappearing act.

We'd had a busy week dealing with chupacabra sightings on the northside that turned out to be coyotes. Then we got a call from the management at the St. Anthony Hotel. Their resident poltergeist was having way too much fun at the Shriners' convention.

For the third time in as many months, I had a "conversation" with the St. Anthony spook, but I was one step away from launching a preemptive exorcism on his butt.

When I climbed the stairs to my office, I found everyone waiting for me to start the morning meeting — including Dex.

"Nice of you to come home," I said, trying my damnedest not to growl. I even stopped and gave him a kiss, which I guess he took as a hopeful sign because I got *his* slow, lazy grin.

Yeah, that's the look that does it for me. Dex can make my heart flip-flop in my chest even when I'm mad enough to rip his head off.

"Sorry, honey," he said. "I had to meet a guy about a thing."

"We'll talk about that later," I said, giving him a look that told him I wasn't buying that tired old line.

I knew Johnny heard the exchange with those vampire-bat ears of his, and I'm pretty sure Ruth picked up on it as well, but both of them had the good grace to feign ignorance.

Then Johnny had to go and say the one thing guaranteed to piss me off.

"We have a client in the waiting area who came to us via the *Texas Monthly* article."

There happened to be a copy of said magazine on my desk, which I picked up and hurled in his direction with some pointed language questioning his parentage.

Vampires have annoying ways of dealing with human temper tantrums. Johnny's hand shot up, and he plucked the periodical out of mid-air. Then, I'll be damned if *he* didn't grin and turn on the urbane bloodsucker charm, which only pissed me off more.

"You are simply beguiling when you lose your temper, dear Selby," he purred.

I searched for a heavier missile and then stopped myself. Playing one-sided catch with an undead immortal stacks up as a zero-sum game in anyone's book.

"Talking to that damned reporter was a mistake," I said in a toneless, level voice.

Johnny sighed. "*Mademoiselle* Sublett allowed the feline to escape the sack," he said. "We had no choice but to attempt to recapture it."

Mary Sue Sublett. The Queen of Whine. Emily Montrose's roommate. The genius who decided playing with a Ouija board was a good idea, thus attracting the attention of the Shadow Man in the first place.

Oh, and the squealer who complained to her rich Daddy that Ruth had taken up with a "devil lady" — that would be me — thus setting in motion the chain of events that led to Ruth leaving her job.

Okay, I owed the teenage pain in the ass for that one. Ruth might have been raking in a good salary at the school, but her talents were wasted.

Being instrumental in getting the headmistress axed sent Mary Sue on a massive power trip. She did a circuit on the religious talk shows "witnessing" about her "struggle with Lucifer" that ended in Emily's murder.

The brat caught the attention of a freelance writer who did a piece on the school. When the guy asked for an interview, I didn't want to do it, but Johnny insisted I sit down with him.

> *"We're supposed to stay off the radar, remember?" I had pointed out to the vampire. "Your rule."*
>
> *Johnny smiled, revealing a row of perfect white teeth — two of them more pointy than the others.*
>
> *"Under normal circumstances you would be correct, darling Selby, but we must also think of our expenses."*
>
> *"What's the matter?" I purred sarcastically. "You skim too much plasma cream off the blood bags this month?*

Johnny bankrolls Selby Jensen Investigations. Arguing finances with him never puts me on firm ground. Even though he made his original fortune in the market before the '29 crash and now runs a profitable string of blood banks, as a businessman, Johnny always looks for ways to improve the bottom line.

He made two arguments in favor of granting the interview whose wisdom I grudgingly admitted. Diversification protects income streams, *and* we didn't know when or *if* any of the Shadow Man's sleeper army of offspring might move against us.

Working on available liquid assets while safeguarding our main resources made for a solid long-term strategy.

Don't worry, I got in plenty of zingers with Johnny's use of the word "liquid." Coming from a vampire that was low-hanging fruit even I couldn't resist.

The other benefit of cooperating with the interview was the opportunity it afforded us to influence the spin the writer put on the story. While we did successfully get rid of the Big Bad at the school, we also had to stick by the official explanation of the crime.

The boiler guy did it in the basement with a pipe.

What neither of us anticipated was how much paranormal flavor the talented freelancer could weave into the "real story" given the history of the buildings that housed the school.

Since the issue of *Texas Monthly* hit the newsstands, we had been flooded with a steady stream of potential clients falling under what Helen called the "Things That Go Bump in the Night Category."

Normally Helen would have been hovering ringside during our morning meeting, but there was a shoe sale at the Saks in North Star Mall. Helen couldn't buy new kicks, but I expected her to come home with something anyway. One of the many things she couldn't explain to me about life on the other side.

Anyway, back to the point. Every living kook and homeless spook in Texas had been showing up on our doorstep for two months. For the most part, I was taking the attitude "if the check cashes, what the hell," but my patience had started to wear thin.

Yes, I had been paid to hunt chupacabra / urban coyotes, turn the screws on the St. Anthony poltergeist, and speak with President Teddy Roosevelt's ghost over at the Menger Hotel.

(Teddy recruited the Rough Riders, also known as the 1st United States Volunteer Cavalry, in that bar in 1898. The President and his men had a grand old time fighting in the Spanish-American War, which has left Teddy with a lingering fondness for the hotel now that he's on the other side.)

But pay or not, I had not enjoyed the demon goat job, nor do

I ever want to hear the word "product" again after staking out a "haunted" beauty parlor — excuse me, "spa and salon" — for a week only to conclude the "restless spirit" was air in the pipes.

Profit margin or not, there are *real monsters* demanding our attention. I get it that Johnny worries most of our cases are *pro bono* but making me sit through one more nut job client interview had the potential to elevate "bail money for Selby" to the top of our expense column.

But then I didn't count on that client being Olivia Reynolds.

5

The voices behind the office door rose and fell in the rhythm of an argument — one heated and impatient, the other cool and reasoning.

"Damn it, Johnny, enough already with the Texas Monthly *clients. You've got some goddamn nerve after that freaking* goat exorcism *to ask me to talk to another one of these people."*

"This woman is not like that Selby. She has traveled from Massachusetts to speak with us, and her story is most unique."

Olivia closed her eyes.

Traveled from Massachusetts.

The phrase sounded like the way someone would describe the beginning of a pleasant summer vacation, not a last-ditch trek into the unknown.

Her "travels" had begun the day before at 6 o'clock in the morning when she stepped off the Logan Express bus and into the hurried bustle of an international airport waking for the day.

The line at the Transportation Security Administration checkpoint snaked back on itself leaving Olivia feeling exposed and visible as she waited to present her driver's license and boarding pass.

None of the other half-awake people in line noticed her, but Olivia watched them with wary caution, the memory of the man at the cemetery never far from her thoughts.

She'd gone straight home from the graveyard, booked a flight, and packed — spending the rest of the night in a chair by the window watching the street and jumping at every sound.

When it was time to leave for the bus, Olivia called for a taxi to drive her to the station, locked her door, and left a note for the landlady with an extra month's rent.

Now, standing in the TSA line, she watched professional business travelers with wheeled bags and young people with backpacks like they could be mortal threats.

Olivia's logical mind told her she was safe in the crowded airport, but she still felt the weight of unseen eyes tracking her movements. Nervously scanning the waiting area again, she noticed a tall man who bore a striking resemblance to the actor Sam Elliott.

Dressed in jeans and biker boots, he had that aura of "bad boy" that appealed to Olivia. "*Maybe I haven't completely lost my mind,*" she thought. "*At least I can still appreciate a good-looking man.*"

Her attention snapped back to the present when the agent said, "Step forward, *please*." From the emphasis on the words, Olivia knew he was repeating himself.

"Sorry," she mumbled, presenting her documents. "Haven't had my coffee yet."

The agent nodded as if he understood, then touched his temple with his index finger. "You mind taking those off?"

Olivia felt her face grow warmer as she fumbled with her dark glasses. "Sorry," she said, blinking painfully in the light. "I forgot I was wearing them."

The man stared at her, probably trying to decide if she really was sleep deprived, hungover, or both. "Something wrong with your eyes?"

"I'm getting over an infection," she lied. "Bright lights are painful."

For a panicked second, Olivia thought she'd aroused official suspicion, but then the agent returned her license and said, "That's too bad. Hope it clears up. Have a good trip."

Olivia thanked him, quickly claiming a bin for her shoes and the contents of her pockets. She wanted away from the press of people and longed for the security of a wall against her back.

As her luggage rolled out of sight on the conveyor belt, Olivia stepped into the circular X-ray machine and raised her arms over her head.

The woman monitoring the device motioned Olivia forward, then held up her hand.

"I'm going to need to pat you down," she said, snapping on a pair of latex gloves. "I'll only use the backs of my hands. Would you prefer a private room?"

Olivia would have preferred not be touched at all but clenched her jaw against the invasion of her personal space.

"No, thank you," she said. "I'm good. Go ahead."

When the woman's gloved hands touched her body, Olivia smelled seawater and heard gulls crying in the distance.

Three more days to the beach. God just get me through three more days.

"Sorry. Your jeans are baggy," the agent said. "They threw the scanner off. Have a nice day."

"You, too," Olivia said, "and have a good time at the beach."

The uniform woman frowned. "How did you know I'm going to the beach?"

"Lucky guess," Olivia said. "You look like you need a break."

"You have no idea," the agent muttered under her breath. "Safe travels."

Olivia moved to a nearby bench to put on her shoes before following her nose to a coffee shop. She counted out the last of her change to pay for a sausage breakfast sandwich and a small coffee, overwhelmed by a sudden, insatiable need for meat.

Mildly disgusted by the greasy bag in her hand, Olivia claimed one of the white rocking chairs by the plate glass windows. She angled the chair to watch both the tarmac and the terminal while she wolfed down the food.

"If my vegan friends could see me now, they'd string me up with eco-friendly rope," she thought, blowing on the coffee before she took a sip.

Uncertainty gnawed at her gut more than hunger. Was this trip to Texas a fool's errand? Would this woman she'd never met take one look at her and decide she was a lunatic?

Olivia planned to use a magazine article as her excuse for her visit because the truth really would make her sound insane.

"Uh, hi. According to this online genealogy site, I think our mothers were sisters. Oh, and I've been having these visionary dreams about our scary gypsy grandmother. Let me show you this book I dug up at her gravesite."

Olivia rested her head in her hands. She still couldn't believe the course her life had taken over the past few months. Steadily increasing physical symptoms. The loss of her job and benefits. A vague diagnosis from multiple doctors of "an autoimmune disorder."

As her health deteriorated, Olivia's life shrank to the confines of her apartment with heavy drapes holding back the blinding sun. Finally, when her muscles ached with such intensity a walk across the room left her crying in pain, Olivia made a decision.

If the medical community couldn't — or wouldn't — help her, she'd help herself. She turned to a healthy diet and began to meditate, but to her dismay, Olivia didn't find the Zen state she sought. Instead, her mind wandered down dark and winding passageways.

Flashes of a small town she'd never seen shattered her concentration. A sticky, humid wind played at her skin, pulling her back to full consciousness parched and gasping.

When turning inward didn't calm her mind, she tried exercise, pushing her aching body until the soreness receded and a new strength infused her muscles. Olivia liked the camaraderie of the gym, but that refuge proved short-lived as well.

The stares of the other weightlifters drove her away after she absently picked up a 100 lb. weight as if it were a feather. She knew she wasn't normal and sensed the dangers of others knowing it as well.

Olivia didn't go back, grappling alone with the increasing belief that her body had begun to transform. The idea scared her, but not nearly as much as her growing craving for the changes to accelerate. The question that tormented her thoughts wasn't, "Who am I?" but rather, "*What* am I?

Adopted at age nine, Olivia knew virtually nothing about her birth family — her parents' names, the vague memory of a severe grandmother dressed in black, her gray hair pulled into a tight bun. Could her family history give her the answers she needed?

Hoping to make the research go faster, Olivia joined a genealogy site online and ordered a DNA test — which she flunked.

The lab said the results were corrupted, but for "unstipulated" reasons, the company refused to allow her to try again.

With the refund she received, Olivia opted for another service that collaborated with the genealogy site. Their test was more expensive, but also more sophisticated. This time, a representative from the company called to apologize.

"Ms. Reynolds, we are so sorry," the voice on the other end of the phone said. "Your sample must have been contaminated during processing."

"Here we go again," Olivia thought, but what she said was, "Why do you think that?"

There was a slight hesitation on the line, and then the woman replied with a chuckle, "The sample we tested in your name doesn't appear to be human."

A chill passed through Olivia, but she played along, trying to make her fake laugh sound genuine.

"We're going to send you a second test kit for free," the woman went on. "It was probably just a screw up in the lab. I'm sure the next test will come out fine."

But the next test didn't come out "fine." The results were the same, and this company, like the first, declined to test another sample.

Forced to work on name matches alone, Olivia painstakingly built out her family tree. She spent hours studying documents and making connections. In the process, she discovered that her mother had a sister named Elizabeth who gave birth to a daughter named Selby in Crystal City, Texas.

On a hunch, Olivia searched online and found an article in *Texas Monthly* magazine.

Now, sitting at the airport, she turned to the story again in a tattered copy of the publications he pulled from her messenger bag. The worn pages fell open to a lurid tale about a girl's school in San Antonio.

A boiler repairman killed one of the students — or at least he confessed to the murder. The investigation involved a PI named Selby Jensen who worked with the lead detective, Lt. Rich Haversham, in an unspecified capacity.

The writer recounted the grisly death by bludgeoning with careful discretion, but then expanded the article's perspective, relying heavily on material provided by the dead girl's roommate.

In a narrative, thoroughly laced with what Olivia took to be religious hysteria, Mary Sue Sublett talked about what she called "Satan's war on the faithful."

According to the girl, a demon possessed the deceased, Emily Montrose, leading her to suggest experimental communications with a Ouija board.

"The devil tried to pull me in, too," Mary Sue said, *"but the power of the sweet Baby Jesus saved me. But poor Emily started going down to that basement talking to a lady in blue she thought was the Virgin Mary. Her faith just wasn't strong enough to know that Lucifer disguises himself in beautiful forms."*

The author used the girl's story as a jumping off point to explore the background of the building that housed the Christian educational institution, uncovering a long history of supposed paranormal activity.

Before the current owners took control of the property, it had been a Catholic girls school and orphanage. Going even further back, the house belonged to a wealthy eccentric who willed it to the Church with the stipulation that his only daughter be allowed to live there for the duration of her life.

"According to people familiar with the property," the article read, *"The spirit of Almira Thurston has never left her beloved home. Wearing the attire of a conventional turn-of-the-century librarian complete with a long, sweeping skirt, her hair done up in a bun, the woman's specter still walks the school's upper halls. Miss Thurston is perhaps the only witness who could provide full testimony to the dark deeds that have transpired in this cursed building, but alas, the dead tell no tales."*

In the center of the next page a photo of a strong-looking woman with dark hair dressed in a black leather jacket and form-fitting jeans looked out at the reader: Selby Jensen.

Olivia ran her fingers over the photograph. How many times she'd held it up to her face in front of the bathroom mirror looking for signs of a familial resemblance. She was convinced this woman was her cousin — and someone who could help Olivia understand what was happening to her.

Scanning the page, Olivia read Selby's terse, grounded response to Mary Sue's hyperbole. *"Miss Sublett has an active imagination. Her roommate's murder pushed that tendency to the limits. The boiler repairman killed the girl in the basement with a pipe. Case closed."*

The author's research cast a different light on Selby's involvement in the case. *"A private investigator well known to local authorities, Jensen has long been associated with unusual occurrences where questions remain unanswered even in the face of convenient explanations."*

In her gut Olivia knew Selby would help her. Something was seriously wrong — or maybe completely right — with Olivia, and she knew that something was no autoimmune disease.

"*Mademoiselle* Reynolds?"

Opening her eyes, Olivia looked up into the face of Selby's business associate, Jonathan Devereaux.

"Forgive me," the man said in his lightly accented English. "We are ready to speak with you."

6

While Johnny and I bickered the rest of the team watched. Ruth sat in a chair in front of my desk. Dex leaned against one of the wide brick ledges at the base of the front windows. Ernest lurked in a corner passing himself off as a sooty rhododendron — his way of staying out of the line of fire.

After one particularly barbed exchange, Ruth caught my eye. Chronologically Ruth and I haven't known one another long, but if you believe all that metaphysical shit — which I have to, given my profession — we're two old souls who have reunited for the next round of incarnation.

"He's not the one you're mad at," she telegraphed to me. *"Listen to him."*

It's in Ruth's nature to be a diplomat, but she also has a soft spot for Johnny. If the vampire had his way, the two of them would be an item, but their relationship hit a major stumbling block almost immediately.

Ruth is a descendent of Johnny's long dead brother-in-law Julien Beauchene.

Granted a *distant* descendant, but there's no getting past the fact that Johnny and Ruth are technically related.

Sometime around 1812 a vampire turned Johnny and tried to turn his wife, Josette. Johnny killed the woman he loved rather than see her condemned to an eternity of bloodsucking.

Here's the kicker. Ruth looks exactly like Josette.

Johnny carries a portrait of his late wife in the lid of his antique gold pocket watch. The first time he showed the likeness to me, I tried to pass the resemblance off as a coincidence, but Johnny wasn't having it.

Don't jump to conclusions. That's not why Johnny fell for Ruth. He's not that cliché. He believes the two of them share a destiny.

Normally I'd be tempted to roll my eyes at that but having my resurrected dead husband back in my life hasn't left me nearly as much room for cynicism as I'd like.

Even I have to admit that Johnny and Ruth are made for each other. For one thing, she doesn't see him being dead as a deal breaker.

The day I introduced them, she did this whole Old Court vampire etiquette thing, offering him her eyes and her bared throat. He didn't bite — literally — which took her off his meal card and placed her under his protection. There are worse ways to start a relationship.

But then Johnny confessed what he had discovered about her connection to Julien and asked Ruth to participate in a séance. We're talking dark room, round table, joined hands – the whole clairvoyant shebang.

Johnny got what he wanted – his dead wife's forgiveness and her thanks for freeing her soul. Josette also gave Johnny her blessing to pursue a new love.

What he wasn't counting on, however, was Ruth's shock at how much she truly is the mirror image of Josette. Not just in looks, but in mannerism and even tone of voice. Understandably, the realization shook her confidence in Johnny's true motivations for being interested in her.

Ruth didn't exactly push Johnny away, but she did markedly slow their forward momentum. Somewhat wounded, Johnny asked me if I thought the family connection caused her to pull back.

You can always count on me to skip straight to the practicalities.

"You're dead. You can't father children. I don't think Ruth is worried about dating her uncle."

(Turns out I jumped to biological conclusions about a vampire siring children, but keep reading, we'll get to that.)

"But you do have a theory about her concerns?" he pressed.

Even at well past 200 years of age, Johnny can still manage to be an obtuse man.

"For Christ's sake, Johnny," I said, "just look at the picture in your damned watch. You're going to have to prove to the woman that you want *her*, not the living memory of your dead wife."

From the stunned look on his face, that idea never occurred to him. How he responded to my statement revealed the quality of the man inside the vampire.

"Every man must prove his worth to the woman he loves," he said with grave sincerity. "I can do that."

All that flashed through my mind in a nanosecond when Ruth silently signaled me to stand down and hear Johnny out. He hadn't brought any of the *Texas Monthly* cases to me for the sheer pleasure of irritating me.

Okay, the *goat exorcism* was to irritate me, but not the others.

Heeding Ruth's advice, I took a breath and said, "What makes this Olivia Reynolds different?"

"As I said," Johnny replied, "she has flown to Texas from Massachusetts specifically to speak with us."

That part of the prospective client's story did intrigue me. I have connections in Boston.

A few years ago, I went up to do a consult on Georges Island. The wife of a captured Confederate soldier haunts the place — understandable since the Yankees hanged her.

My colleague, Blackie O'Reilly, could not get it through to the spirit that the Civil War ended a long time ago. I explained to her, as gently as possible, that the outcome is called the "Lost" Cause for a reason.

The news went over about like the first cannon shot at Fort Sumter, but at least I had the right accent. We spent half the night commiserating about the "treachery of northern aggression" and then struck a bargain.

She's allowed to wander around with her lantern, yell a few threats when people visit the dungeon, and even tap the occasional tourist on the shoulder. Choking the living, however, is off the table.

Before the night ended, the ghost revealed to me the true reason for her unrest. The Yankees didn't kill her husband; she did. During the escape attempt her gun went off by accident.

More times than not when you get to know a restless soul you can drill down to the source of their pain. For a few, that's enough to help them move on. The Confederate lady wasn't that lucky, but she's doing a better job managing her anger.

"Why did this Reynolds woman come all the way to Texas to talk to us?" I asked. "Boston has one of the biggest ghost populations in America. Paranormal investigators are a dime a dozen up there."

"*Oui*," Johnny agreed, "but when she read the *Texas Monthly* article, *Mademoiselle* Reynolds came to believe that only our team could be of assistance to her."

"Why was somebody in Massachusetts be reading *Texas*

Monthly?" I asked. "That doesn't make a lot of sense to me. What are you not telling me about this woman?"

With uncharacteristic reticence he said, "I am drawn to her in a way I cannot explain. She feels familiar although I am certain we have never met. As a favor to me, Selby, please speak with her."

Johnny almost never calls in a favor. I gave in — maybe not with rabid enthusiasm — but more willing than when our conversation began.

~

JOHNNY USHERED A SLIGHTLY BUILT woman with reddish brown hair and a pale complexion into the office. Even though I was sure the vampire had put the idea in my head, there did seem to be something familiar about her.

Olivia took the chair across from Ruth, hesitated, and removed her celebrity-sized sunglasses, blinking painfully. We tinted the windows in the building in deference to Johnny's light issues, but the room obviously wasn't dim enough for our prospective client.

"Would you mind?" she asked, gesturing toward the blinds. Dex quietly worked the mechanism while Johnny took care of the introductions.

Once our surroundings had been plunged into mid-winter gloom, I got right to the point. "How can we help you, Ms. Reynolds? Johnny tells me you've come a long way to see us."

The woman nodded, answering me in a stronger, richer voice than I anticipated. "I've been traveling for two days," she said. "I slept in the airport in Utah last night. Now that I'm finally here, I don't know where to start."

Johnny intervened. "Perhaps you should recount your story to Selby as you shared it with me."

A smile tugged at the corners of Olivia's mouth. She visibly relaxed. Johnny's speech pattern does that to women.

"I haven't been well," she began, launching into a recitation about doctor's visits and lab tests that made my skin crawl. I don't do doctors unless there's blood or broken bones involved — and sometimes not even then.

As soon as she got to the part about the DNA tests, I cut my eyes toward Johnny. The vampire tried to look innocent and failed. No wonder he wanted to take the case. Blood is his thing.

By the third "contaminated" test, I'd started to doodle a few notes on the pad in front of me. Then she talked about losing her benefits and my blood began to boil. I despise insurance companies. Biggest confidence game in the nation. Bottom line, sick people get screwed every day in America so those bastards can make a profit.

For 18 months the woman sitting in front of me slogged through life feeling like shit while a bunch of bureaucrats made decisions about her life. Autoimmune disorder my ass. I didn't know what was wrong with Olivia Reynolds, but I did know that if anyone could figure it out, Johnny could.

Still, my spidey sense told me Olivia Reynolds hadn't come clean about everything, a suspicion I immediately put on the table.

"What's the rest of the story?" I asked.

She smiled — really smiled — an expression I could tell Olivia hadn't used much lately. The woman liked that I'd detected the holes in her story.

"The article on the murder at the girl's school said you were involved with the DNA analysis of the evidence. Go over my DNA results and give me your professional opinion, then I'll tell you the rest."

So, the lady knew how to play poker. She'd just raised the bet.

"You know we're not doctors," I cautioned.

"I do," Olivia said, "but the magazine article suggested you color outside the lines."

Everyone in the room burst out laughing, winning a rotating glare from me. I didn't even spare Ernest, whose leaves shook with barely suppressed mirth. I caught Olivia looking at the "plant," but she didn't say anything.

"Enough with the death stare, Selby," Dex laughed, wiping tears from his eyes. "You couldn't color inside the lines if you wanted to. You're the only person I know who has authority issues with crayons."

Considering how mad I was at him already, the man was taking his life in his hands, but I decided that ripping my husband a new one in front of a client wasn't a good management technique.

Looking back at Olivia, I shrugged, "Busted," I admitted. "I've got a thing about lines."

"So do I," she said. "That's why I'm here."

We eyed one another silently. What the heck was it about this woman that tugged at my memory?

"Let's say we do get to the point of full disclosure," I said. "What do you expect us to do then?"

Expectations are land mines waiting to go off. I like to know where they're sitting on the playing field.

"*If* we get to that point," Olivia said, "I expect you to help me get answers to questions that other people seem to be afraid to ask."

Well played, Lady from Massachusetts. Well played. I called her bet and shoved our chips in the game.

"Okay. Blood analysis is your department, Johnny. I'm guessing you're in?"

"Indeed," he said, "but to give you my best opinion, *Mademoi-*

selle Reynolds I must draw blood rather than collect a saliva sample. Would that be acceptable?"

"Olivia," she said. "If I'm going to open a vein for someone, they get to use my first name."

This time, no one dared laugh. We couldn't have explained why the idea of Olivia opening a vein for Johnny was funny.

Instead, I assured her with mock but convincing gravity, "You're in good hands. There's no one better with blood than Johnny."

7

Ruth took charge of Olivia and came to a rapid conclusion; the woman wasn't down on her luck, she was flat broke. While Johnny drew the blood samples in his lab downstairs, Ruth pulled me out in the hall.

"She spent every dime she had flying here from New England," she whispered. "Olivia confessed to me that she can pay your retainer, but she can't afford a hotel. She's planning to sleep at the Y."

Some plan. Straight out of a bad "B" movie.

"Is the Y even a thing anymore?" I asked.

"I have absolutely no idea," Ruth replied, "but that doesn't matter anyway. Olivia isn't well. We have to put her up in one of the extra rooms here."

Notice there was no question in there anywhere.

"And what if she sees something here we can't explain?" I asked. "Bunking with us is like staying over with the Munsters."

From the doorway to the lab, Johnny said, "If my suspicions are correct, we may have to reveal our true natures to our guest immediately."

Judging from the expression on his face, Olivia was going to have to show us her cards as well.

"You have the test results already?" I said. "How the hell did you pull that off? You just drew her blood."

When he answered, Johnny's voice dropped to a lower register and something otherworldly moved across his eyes.

"The machines will deliver the results in approximately four hours. My suppositions are more personal in nature. You must understand that while I have cultivated the discipline to draw samples for scientific purposes, the task presents challenges. The scent of living blood awakens my senses."

By vampire standards, Johnny qualifies as a young man, but to us, he's old. Living in the modern world and playing with technological toys doesn't change that. When he drops the carefully crafted, glib persona and goes all Count Darkness? The situation shifts into serious gear.

"Out with it, Johnny."

"Her blood whispers to me," he said. "We share kinship."

Ruth and I exchanged a look. He couldn't possibly be saying what it sounded like he was saying.

"Olivia can't be a vampire," Ruth said. "She came to us in daylight."

Johnny shook his head. "She is not a vampire," he agreed. "She is something far more rare and potentially dangerous. I believe her to be a dhampir."

Don't feel bad. I had to get a definition, too.

A dhampir is a child born of the union of a male vampire and a female human.

What the hell had we gotten ourselves into this time?

Olivia reluctantly, but gratefully accepted Ruth's invitation to take one of the empty offices in our building. We keep a couple of rooms outfitted with basic furniture for situations like hers. It's not the Ritz, but it is free, which matters more than thread count.

Confessing complete exhaustion after 48 hours of hard travel, she went down for a nap. In her place, I wouldn't have been on my feet at all. Look at a map and explain to me how in the hell anyone came up with a route between Massachusetts and Texas that involves Utah.

Anyway, when Johnny's machines finished the analysis, he came upstairs armed with printouts and laid out the science for Ruth and me.

I'll spare you the subsequent 30-minute lecture complete with diagrams on the whiteboard. Long story short; he wasn't wrong.

"We must take this to Don Eugenio," he said. "I am honor bound to disclose to him the existence of a dhampir in his city."

(First, let's take a pronunciation break here. I doubt you're ever going to meet the Don, but if you do, don't called him "U-gene-io." He doesn't like that. At *all*. The correct way to say his name is "A-u-hane-io.")

Don Eugenio Seguín controls all of Texas south of San Antonio for a good reason; he's been here since the city was founded in 1718.

The vampires in the Lone Star State don't give a crap that General Sam Houston, venerated hero of the Texas Revolution and the first president of the Republic of Texas, pulled off a major land grab at the Battle of San Jacinto in 1836.

That's where General Sam put a Bowie knife to Mexican President Antonio López de Santa Anna's jugular vein. You ever seen a Bowie knife? The blade is 8 inches long and 2 inches thick.

When Houston suggested that the Rio Grande should be the

southern border of Texas, El Presidente offered a prudent, "Sí," redrawing the boundary lines and bringing an end to the Texas Revolution.

While the humans set about forming a Republic, the vampires stuck to business as usual, maintaining their customary territorial claims. But when Texas became part of the United States in 1845, Don Eugenio refused to bring his people into the American vampiric political structure.

He told me once that he saw the American Civil War coming and wanted no part of it. Had he agreed to annex his holdings as an American vampire territory, he would have been forced to choose sides in the coming war. As a staunch opponent of slavery that would have put his people in a hell of a position.

Human historians have no idea the intricate supernatural politics that never make it into the official record.

There were plenty of bloodsuckers among the first settlers to the New World; vampires who broke away from the Old Court in Europe and came to America looking for their own version of "religious" freedom.

They, like their human counterparts, ultimately adopted a reasonably democratic governmental structure. In modern times they divide the country into territories ruled by governors who are generally the oldest vampires in the region.

Within the territories, master vampires oversee major cities where they maintain the rule of law. Except in Texas. Here, at least from San Antonio south, Don Eugenio is the *patrón*.

Johnny has no taste for politics, but he's a stickler for manners. He owes allegiance to the Undead Godfather and so do I.

If Don Eugenio wanted to drive someone like me out of his city, he could, but thankfully he sees me as an asset, an occasional drinking buddy, and a friend.

Nobody, and I mean nobody, has a more hollow leg for

tequila than a vampire nearing the 1,000-year mark. Especially one who controls most of the agave production in Mexico.

We have a personal connection, but I'll get to that. For now, understand that in a roundabout way, Don Eugenio funds a major part of our business. Johnny's blood bank, or as I like to call it, McDracula's, has most-favored platelet status with the Don and his lieutenants.

They pay top shelf prices, which allows us to do *pro bono* paranormal pest control mostly unfettered by budgetary shortfalls.

There are *quid pro quo* aspects to the arrangement. If something comes to our attention that would disrupt the smooth operations of Don Eugenio's world, we're obligated to let him know.

Mainstream American vampires, even ancient ones like the Don, prefer to lead quiet lives off the grid. Fewer episodes of villagers with torches and pitchforks that way.

The breakdown of conventional social ties in the 21st century serves vamps well. These days reclusive behavior never arouses suspicion before the fact.

It's only after something happens that the neighbors look into the news cameras and say, "He kept to himself and didn't have anything to do with other people."

Cue the high school teacher talking about how the suspect had a thing for *Catcher in the Rye* and was a lone wolf introvert.

(If you buy that bullshit stereotype about all introverts being sociopaths in the making, I'm one frayed nerve ending away from a psychotic break.)

Vampires go to great lengths to ensure they are never the subject of such reports. They tend to work from home, manage their dietary concerns in non-lethal ways, and many actively contribute to human society.

I can't tell you how many papers on hematology Johnny has

published. He's involved in research projects around the globe without ever leaving the comfort of our basement.

There's a difference between *hiding* well and *living* well while you're doing it. If you're going to be around forever battling the inescapable loneliness of that fate, having a purpose goes a long way toward making the centuries pass faster.

Having put down more than one rogue vampire at the Don's behest, I fully understood the implications of that threat, but I knew nothing about dhampirs.

"Of course, we'll take this to the Don," I told Johnny, "but first, get me up to speed. How unique are dhampirs?"

"Olivia is the only one whose existence has ever been confirmed so far as I know," he replied.

Unique creatures rarely lead undisturbed lives, mainly because there's always some bastard looking to puff up his ego by killing them.

"How much danger does that present for Olivia?" Ruth asked.

"A great deal," Johnny said. "For as long as my kind have walked the earth, there are those who have sought if not a cure, at least a means to normalize our existence."

That motivation explains Johnny's preoccupation with hematology. He regards vampirism as a disease that might be reversible.

"Should word of Olivia's nature spread in vampire society and reach the power brokers of Europe," he went on, "she will be regarded as a legend come to life. Many scientists will seek to study her with or without her permission. I cannot guarantee the purity of their purpose, particularly among the members of the Old Court."

"You've been looking for a cure for as long as I've known you," I said. "What if Olivia is the key to that?"

He rotated his laptop so that I could see the screen. "This," he said, opening an image, "is a chemical profile of my blood, and this is Olivia's."

"Okay," I said slowly, "since I have no idea what I'm supposed to be looking at, I'll take your word for that."

"Vampire DNA functions in the same way as human DNA," Johnny said. "When a new vampire is sired, additional DNA is introduced into their system, where it behaves after the fashion of a virus. The new DNA has genes that impart vampiric traits to the human. Olivia did not inherit all of those genes, so the presentation of what you might call the 'symptoms' of vampirism are unique."

"Okay, so does that mean you can develop a cure from her blood?"

"It is impossible at this time to say," Johnny said, giving us one of those Gallic shrugs that looks nonchalant but means the shit is about to make contact with the rotary device.

"*But?*" I prompted.

"Her blood does seem to have the capacity to alter mine."

This conversation was like pulling fangs. "Alter it *how*, Johnny?" I asked impatiently.

"You are aware of what occurs when my blood is exposed to full sunshine?" he asked.

"It boils," I replied.

"Correct, but when mixed with Olivia's blood, my sample remains stable when subjected to intense sunlight."

Holy *crap.*

"Then Olivia does hold the potential for a cure?"

"We must not get ahead of ourselves in that regard," he said. "The reaction of Olivia's blood to mine does not follow the scientific behavior of inherited traits. There is much more to be discovered in her DNA, a process that will not be so benign should she become the subject of experiments outside our control."

A nice way of saying that in the wrong hands, Olivia would be turned into a lab rat with a permanent needle stuck in her arm.

Ruth, who had been studying Johnny's face, said thoughtfully, "You don't think she could be the source of a cure. You're wondering about some kind of temporary antidote."

The vampire's eyes came alive with admiration. "In theory, her metabolism might contain the key to a compound that would convey temporary and partial immunity from one or more aspects of vampirism."

"Which other aspects?" I asked.

When he reached for his printouts, I added, "In English."

"If I am to supply a hypothetical response to that question, *Mademoiselle* Reynolds must share with us the remainder of her story. As I said, I have lingering questions regarding her heritage."

Well, that settled that. It was time to wake Sleeping Beauty.

8

Ruth ordered supper from a nearby restaurant. While Dex retrieved the food, she covered the conference table with a white cloth. We all gathered at about 6 o'clock to simultaneously break bread and bad news.

Even though Johnny doesn't eat, he spared our digestion and waited to discuss his findings until we pushed our plates away. Ernest maintained his rhododendron disguise and Helen, freshly returned from the mall, hovered near the ceiling sporting a new pair of Manolo Blahnik's.

When she blipped in earlier, I took one look at her footwear and said, "Please tell me you didn't steal those."

"Selby, I'm a ghost, how could I possibly shoplift?" she replied, all bright eyed and innocent.

"I don't know," I countered, "are you telling me you paid for them?"

Her brow creased. "No," she admitted, "I didn't."

"Then how did they get on your feet?"

Helen's frown deepened. "I just stare at stuff in the stores. If I do it long enough and hard enough then all of a sudden I'm wearing it."

We'd had many variations of this conversation through the years. None of us — especially Helen herself — had a plausible explanation for her post mortem shopping abilities.

In the end, I decided yet again to let the question remain one of life's great mysteries. God knows Helen would never have been able to afford those shoes when she was alive. Her retail acquisitions are a death benefit that keeps on giving.

Switching topics, I filled Helen in on Olivia's situation.

"Good Lord," she said, "after everything this poor woman has been through now you're going to have to tell her that her Dad was Dracula? That sucks."

Grimacing at the lame joke, I leaned back in my chair and looked at my dead bestie perched on the edge of my desk. "Something tells me Olivia may not be as surprised about that information as you might think," I said.

"You're kidding," Helen said, amusing herself by levitating the pencils I kept in a Mason jar by the phone.

"I'm not," I said, snatching the yellow number twos out of thin air and replacing them in the jar. "Olivia didn't go to one of those companies that screen for genetic diseases first. She took a test from a genealogy service. That means she had questions about her family tree."

Helen shrugged, turning her attention to the stapler, which she threw into a series of looping somersaults. "She could probably get the test cheaper," she shrugged.

I caught the stapler with my left hand. "What are you?" I said. "The ADHD apparition? Stop playing with my desk accessories."

"Sorry," she said, her luminescence intensifying in a sort of ectoplasmic hot flash. "Being that close to so much killer footwear gets me all juiced up and nervous. I mean, what if I picked the wrong pair?"

"My sympathies," I demurred. "Flying pencils and staplers make *me* nervous, so knock it off."

Folding her hands primly in her lap, Helen said, "Go on. What's your theory about why she took a genealogy DNA test?"

"Like I said, she must have had suspicions about her family. I imagine she was looking for a genetic connection to her illness, which is going to complicate the hell out of things if one exists. One dhampir will be hard enough to manage; a litter will be a nightmare."

Color me the Princess of Understatement.

An hour and a half later, when supper was over, I took in a long breath and said, "Olivia, Johnny found some interesting things in your DNA results that we'd like to discuss with you."

I had assumed our first hurdle would be convincing Olivia she wasn't crazy, but that's not how the scene played out.

Johnny displayed his DNA findings beside the ones from the two laboratories with which Olivia had worked. I didn't bother to ask him how he got the results from the companies. He's as good with a computer as he is with lab equipment.

When the test panels were lined up even I could see they were identical.

Olivia studied the diagrams and then looked at Johnny. "They weren't wrong, were they?" she asked in a calm voice.

"No," Johnny said. "There was no error. The laboratories simply did not know what to say to you, so they opted for the most plausible excuse: contamination."

A look of hope washed across the woman's pale face. "But you do know what to say, don't you?"

Johnny caught my eye, tossing the proverbial "ball" in my direction. Gallant leader that I am, I tossed it straight to Ruth.

I'm staring 40 dead in the face. Ruth is 52. The first time I met her she was going by "Mary Ruth" and looked like a buttoned-up school marm.

The second time, here in my office, sensing we were "her kind of people," she dropped the "Mary." Dressed in jeans with her chestnut hair falling down around her shoulders, Ruth looked years younger. She's one of those women who turns silver at the temples into an asset.

No one would call Ruth Beauchene "matronly," but she's definitely the team member with the greatest talent for comforting someone, especially when she slides into the honeyed, fluid accent of her bayou homeland.

Reaching across the table, she caught hold of Olivia's hand. "Yes, *cher*," she said. "We do know what to say to you, but it may be hard for you to hear."

Tears filled Olivia's eyes. "Nothing could be harder than what I've already been through," she said. "Or harder than the decision to come here. I can't explain it, but I knew you'd find an answer for me. If you have, I want to hear it."

As gently as possible, Ruth told her the truth. "Your lab results show that you are the descendant of the union of a vampire and a human."

All things considered, Olivia took the news pretty well.

Okay, first her eyes went round as saucers and she sagged heavily against the back of her chair.

Then she took it well.

"May I have a glass of water, please?" she asked in a small voice.

Dex got it for her.

"Are you sure you don't want something stronger?" he said when he held out the glass.

She shook her head. Her hand trembled as she drained the glass.

"So," she said, making an enormous effort to frame the question as perfectly reasonable, "vampires are real?"

Ruth smiled. "They are real. You're sitting across the table from one."

Olivia's head swiveled back and forth between Ruth and Johnny. After several seconds, her gaze zoomed in on Johnny and she narrowed her eyes. He didn't flinch under her scrutiny. Finally, she said, "I think I see it now."

"What do you see?" he asked.

She concentrated intently. "There's sort of a faint glow around you, right? I have to squint to make it out, but it's there."

Johnny nodded. "It is. Were you a full vampire, you would see the field of my energy as a pale aura."

That was news to me, but Ruth was nodding. "You can see it, too?" I asked, sounding like a kid who didn't get the club decoder ring.

"Yes," Ruth said, "but only in certain lights."

Still staring at Johnny, Olivia asked the standard first question everyone puts to a vampire. "Do you mind telling me how old you are?"

He replied patiently, "I became a creature of the night in 1812. At the time, I was 32 years old. In human terms, I will always be 32."

There was no way I could let an opening that wide just slide on by.

"Give or take a couple of hundred years," I deadpanned.

The wisecrack broke the tension in the room. We all laughed. When the conversation resumed, Olivia seemed to be getting her footing again. "You must be a good man," she said to Johnny.

Cocking his head to the side, the vampire asked, "Why would you say that"

Olivia smiled. "Because of the way Ruth looks at you. I mean, the two of you are an item, right?"

Johnny looked down, a gesture that was both hopeful and mildly embarrassed.

"I do not know if I am a good man," he said softly, "but I can tell you that were I ever to win the hand of a woman such as Ruth Beauchene, I would regard myself as the luckiest of beings — living or dead."

He looked up at Ruth as he said those last words. For just an instant they locked eyes and Ruth let a suggestion of her real feelings for Johnny surface.

Damn.

The two of them can heat up a room when they're not scaring the hell out of each other.

But as quickly as her face betrayed her heart, Ruth's expression returned to pleasant neutrality and she redirected her attention toward Olivia.

"Johnny is a good man," she said. "Bearing the curse of vampirism does not necessarily mean any person is evil. Certainly there are bad vampires, as there are bad humans. Johnny is not a bad vampire."

Answering a question with a non-answer is another one of Ruth's skills.

Olivia considered the statement and then said, in a voice that made her sound small and uncertain, "What am I exactly?"

"The technical term is 'dhampir,'" Johnny replied.

"And I'm not evil?"

Ruth took hold of Olivia's hand again. "Neither of us sense even a suggestion of evil from you," she assured her.

"Are you a . . ." Olivia stopped, not sure how to continue.

Ruth saved her the trouble. "I'm a witch."

"And you?" Olivia asked Dex.

"Just your average corporeal ghost," he replied making the phrase sound as casual as *plumber* or *mechanic*. When he added, "You're good in my book," Olivia gave him a grateful smile.

Her attention tracked to me. "Sorry," I shrugged. "I'm the

token human in the family, but you don't set off any alarms with me, either."

Tilting her head inquisitively, she said, "You're human? I thought with your eyes . . . "

If Ernest hadn't coughed over her words, I would have been forced to come up with something fast. Thankfully, nobody seemed to notice what Olivia had started to say, but I caught Ruth eyeing me closely. The next series of events allowed me to ignore her scrutiny, however, and move on.

First, Olivia said, "Did that plant just make a sound?"

Then, "the plant" dissolved into a column of smoke and floated across the room becoming increasingly humanoid as it moved toward us.

"Hi, I'm Ernest. Resident wildfire elemental. Also a no vote on the evil thing. Nice to meet you."

That did it. Olivia Reynolds passed out cold.

9

"Way to go, Ernest," I said as Ruth moved to tend the unconscious woman.

Indignant sparks erupted from the column of smoke. "Hey!" he exclaimed. "How was I supposed to know a little soot would push her over the edge? She took the vampire/witch/ghost announcements fine."

Before I could argue, Olivia began to regain consciousness. The apologies started as soon as her eyes opened.

"What a ridiculous thing for me to do," she said, struggling to sit up.

Ruth put a restraining hand on her shoulder. "Slow down and get your bearings. We've given you a great deal to process."

Ernest wafted down to the floor beside Olivia and coalesced into the shape of a teddy bear.

As proof that I can practice self-restraint, not one Smokey the Bear crack passed my lips. Remember, only you can prevent bad one liners.

"I'm sorry, lady," Ernest said. "I didn't mean to scare you."

Olivia blinked rapidly a few times and then rose to the occasion. "That's okay . . ."

"Ernest," he said. "Like I said, I'm the resident wildfire elemental."

"I don't know what that means," Olivia admitted.

"Don't worry about it," Ernest replied, emphasizing the words with a burst of cheerful sparks. "You're in paranormal kindergarten. I'm an assignment from the advanced class. You'll catch up."

The miniature fireworks display made our guest flinch, but the words put a smile on her face. Even fire-breathing teddy bears are cute in their own way.

"Is there anyone else here I should know about?" she asked Ruth, bracing herself for any additional surprises.

On cue, Helen slowly appeared, hands held out in placation. "Now don't freak out," she said. "I'm Helen, your garden variety ghost diva."

"Ghost diva?" Olivia repeated weakly.

Brightening, Helen said, "You got it. I refuse to let death cramp my sense of style or keep me out of the mall. I'm Selby's dead BFF. It's a pleasure to meet you."

"Likewise," Olivia murmured as she rose to her feet and reclaimed her chair at the table.

"You okay to go on?" I asked.

"I think so," Olivia said. "I have a lot of questions, but we made a deal. There are things I haven't shared with you about my physical condition that you need to know."

True to her word, she laid the details of her recent health history on the table for us to dissect.

Vivid, visionary dreams. Incidents of accidental telepathy. Heightened sense of smell. Greater physical strength. Overwhelming cravings for red meat.

More than enough to convince anyone they were losing their minds.

Johnny took copious notes and pressed Olivia for greater

details while the rest of us listened. "Does the sun burn your skin or are you merely uncomfortable in bright light?"

"I've always been bad to sunburn," she answered. "I don't notice anything different about that, but bright lights are excruciating. Is that how it is for you?"

"No," Johnny said. "I cannot go out in full sun, but if I am provided with shade and darkened windows, I can venture beyond these walls during the daylight hours. Such an excursion requires considerable forethought, however."

"And your vision?"

"I have superb vision in any light."

"Interesting," she said. "Now that you mention it, I haven't needed my reading glasses for fine print lately."

Johnny made another note. "You mentioned accidental incidents of mind reading," he said. "Has this occurred with humans only?"

"No," Olivia said, "sometimes when I hear birds singing, I can make out words in the notes."

"Fascinating," Johnny said.

She watched him writing for several seconds and then asked, "What can I do to manage my symptoms?"

Johnny put down his pen. "You are not ill. You must no longer think of yourself in those terms. The changes in your physiology are not symptoms, they are gifts."

Before she thought, Olivia blurted out, "How can a craving for raw meat be a gift?"

"Because," Johnny said quietly, "it saves you from a thirst for blood."

There's some tough love for you. Olivia looked so shocked, he might as well have said, "*Pint of O-positive or a sirloin rare? You pick.*"

"But," she stuttered, "do you know what they feed farm

animals? I mean there's antibiotics and growth hormones and . . . and . . . I'm a vegan."

"Those things," Johnny said, "are the least of your concerns."

I swear to you, Olivia looked indignant. "What? I can't be half vampire and care about the environment?"

"Perhaps we can save that philosophical question for a later discussion," Johnny said patiently. "The point I am endeavoring to make is that it would be a grave mistake to deny your body that nutrition it requires."

That did it. Ruth and I both burst out laughing. Johnny looked at us like we'd lost our minds.

"You find the nutritional needs of supernatural creatures amusing?" he asked.

"No," I said, wiping my eyes, "I find a vampire using the phrase 'grave mistake' hysterical."

"*Sacré bleau*," he muttered. "As I was saying, Olivia must eat correctly so as to stabilize her developing abilities. We can more accurately assess the extent to which her dhampirism poses a threat to her safety when we know precisely what she can do."

Well, so much for injecting a levity into the situation.

"I don't understand," Olivia said. "Why would I be in danger?"

There's no easy way to tell someone that a race of immortals would love to get their fangs on you and turn you into their personal lab rat. Johnny did a better job with the news than I would have managed.

"From my initial blood tests," he said, "I have developed a hypothesis that your blood might hold the key to a drug that would temporarily suspend the more debilitating aspects of vampirism, allowing my kind to walk among humans."

Without hesitation, and with a definite note of hope in the words, Olivia said, "But wouldn't that be a *good* thing?"

That's when I realized the depth of our obligation to protect this woman. She clearly hadn't seen enough horror movies in her life. Her mind went straight to the humanitarian angle of dhampirism. Mine instantly imagined a world where immortals with superpowers could walk around in broad daylight.

She saw a cure. I saw a means by which the undead could subjugate the human race.

Think I'm an incurable cynic? Work with me. Give half the world, living or dead, the chance to dominate the other half. What do you think would happen? If you're with Olivia, that optimism is going to get your ass killed.

In the wrong hands, Olivia's blood could give vampires an advantage over humans you can damn well bet the bloodsuckers would use, and honestly, who could blame them? Johnny tried to make her see that.

"If all vampires wished to walk in the light once again purely to feel the warmth of the sun on our faces, yes, the scenario we discuss would be, as you say, a 'good thing,'" Johnny said. "But many vampires no longer feel an affinity for the human race of which we were once a part."

"Why?" Olivia asked.

"We have been hunted for centuries," Johnny explained, "tortured by the church, driven underground to live in the shadows. An opportunity to gain mastery over humans on a grand scale would be a difficult thing for many to pass up. This is why our laws have long forbidden the attempted creation of dhampirs."

Yep. Vampires have laws. I didn't know until that moment that dhampirs were illegal under their system, but I wasn't surprised. As a race, vampires have survived by getting a handle on their less elegant impulses, something we humans don't manage worth a damn. A vampire human hybrid? What could possibly go wrong?

In Olivia's case, a confused woman whose life caved in

around her. But in another person? One of lesser heart and fewer scruples? Yeah. Stay tuned. This story's not over yet.

Warring emotions played over Olivia's features. I saw the exact moment when she realized the extreme vulnerability of her position. All the color drained from her face. Ruth and I exchanged a look. The last thing we needed was for our client to pass out again.

Before either of us could say anything, however, Johnny went back in with more questions, a move that caused Ruth's protective instincts to flare — in French no less.

She spit something out I didn't follow, and Johnny answered in the same language. I couldn't translate what he said, but there was an edge of irritation to the words. His thoughts were on the intriguing genetic puzzle sitting before him, not the human living inside that puzzle.

I held up my hands to head off the Gallic fight in the making. "English, please."

"Olivia needs a good night's rest before we continue this interview," Ruth replied firmly. "We can take this back up in the morning."

Nonplussed, Johnny said, "Our research demands additional data."

Dex caught my attention and shook his head. If both he and Ruth thought Olivia shouldn't go on, that was enough for me.

"We'll reconvene in the morning," I said. "It's been a long day. We could all use some shut eye."

When Johnny started to argue, I cut him short. "You don't need sleep, the rest of us do."

Left to his own devices, Johnny would have kept us there all night, but I saw him pause to take in the tired lines around Olivia's mouth and the dark circles under her eyes — and to gauge the level of Ruth's anger. He opted for the better part of valor and retreated.

"Forgive my enthusiasm," he said. "Selby is correct, I do not require rest. That fact can make me insensitive to the needs of others. I will look forward to continuing this conversation on the morrow, *mademoiselle*."

Olivia would have soldiered on if we'd asked her to, but there was no mistaking the relief that washed over her face.

"I'll be fine in the morning," she assured him. "Then you can ask me as many questions as you like."

Ruth held her hand out to Olivia. "Come on," she said. "I'll walk you to your room."

After they'd exited, I crooked my finger at Ernest. He'd stayed in teddy bear mode throughout the conversation, but now expanded into a smokey column roughly equal to my height.

Looking at what I assumed was his "face," I said, "Keep an eye on Olivia tonight, but don't skulk in corners and scare her doing it."

"No problemo, *jefe*," he replied, manifesting a hand and arm with which he saluted crisply. "I'll go in through the back door."

With that, he disappeared into the nearest air conditioning vent.

As we watched the last charcoal tendril move through the grate, Dex said, "You nervous about something?"

"Not nervous," I said, "cautious. We're dealing with a lot of unknowns. Keeping an eye on her seems like the smart play."

"Agreed," Dex said. "You ready to turn in?"

I looked at Johnny. "Anything else?"

"No," the vampire said. "Given Olivia's description of her emerging powers, I wish to review my findings and perhaps run additional tests with the remaining blood samples. I have more than enough to keep me occupied until morning."

He headed down to his lab and Helen settled in front of the

TV in my office for a marathon of *Real Housewives*. Dex and I started for the stairs, but Ruth caught me in the hall.

"Could I talk to you a minute before you go up?" she asked.

"Sure," I said, turning to Dex. "I'll be there in a minute."

Ruth waited until we heard the apartment door open and close over our heads. Then, in a low voice, she asked, "Is there something we need to discuss?"

"Like what?" I hedged.

At that, Ruth put her back to the brick wall, crossed her arms, and gave me her scary headmistress look. "Like what Olivia thought she saw in your eyes."

I spent a lot of time in the principal's office in my day. I know how to lie without really lying. "She was mistaken. You know as well as I do that I'm human."

Ruth's mouth pursed. "Yes, I know you're a human, one who at the moment is lying to a witch who happens to be your friend."

"Then as my friend, let it go."

Somebody else might have backed off. Ruth didn't.

"When I took this job," she said, "you gave me permission not to buy any of your bullshit. I'm calling bullshit."

Crap. I did say that.

"It's nothing I can't control," I replied warily.

"Do you mind if I verify that?" Ruth asked, holding out her hands.

Reluctantly, I agreed, shivering as her power crawled over me. Completely against my will, something inside me answered before I could stop it.

Ruth's eyes widened. "How long?" she asked.

There was no point in keeping up the ruse. She had me dead to rights.

"Since my father died when I was sixteen years old, but it's been gone a long time."

"And now it's back. When did it return?"

"Sometime after that night at the school. Definitely the first night I woke up and found Dex gone."

The probing magic receded, but Ruth didn't release my hands. "Let me help you."

The strength in her touch and the warmth of the offer brought a lump to my throat. "I will," I said, "but we have too much going on right now. The first chance we get to talk by ourselves, I'll tell you the whole story. I promise."

"I'm going to hold you to that," she said, squeezing my fingers before she released me. "Get some sleep. Something tells me tomorrow will be a long day."

Little did she know I might be facing a long night.

My husband had some explaining to do.

10

When I closed the apartment door, I went straight to the gun cabinet for my cleaning supplies. Dex walked into the kitchen as I began to disassemble the Glock. He took one look at the scene playing out in front of him and knew we were on shaky ground.

Still, he tried to keep things light. I like misguided optimism in a man.

I heard the fridge door open followed by the clink of a longneck and the rattle of a beer cap hitting the rim of the trashcan.

"How are the new grips?" he asked.

"Good," I answered. "Luther tried to sell me a laser sight again."

"He does that to annoy the shit out of you."

"It works," I said, glancing in his direction.

Gesturing with the bottle, Dex said, "You want one?"

"No," I said. "We need to talk."

"I figured as much when you started cleaning your piece."

"I never put a gun up dirty," I said, threading an oiled patch into the slotted tip of the cleaning rod.

"*That* gun you never put up at all," he said. "So, how mad are you?"

"I burned through 200 wadcutters at Luther's."

Dex let out a low whistle. "Guess I better be glad you're cleaning that Glock and not pointing it at me and pulling the trigger."

Running a rag over the barrel, I said, "If I did, would it kill you?"

He shook his head. "Nope, but it would sting."

"I'll remember that."

Dex sat the bottle down and moved to stand behind me, resting his hands on my shoulders. "You're not going to shoot me, Selby," he said. "I'm sorry it scares you when you wake up at night and I'm not here. I'll try not to do that to you anymore."

Damn him. He's always been able to barge straight through my defenses and appeal to my heart. Which I both love and hate about the man. Especially when I need to stay mad at him to get the words out.

I put my tools down, reached up, and rested my hand over his. "When you disappear like that, how do I know you're going to come back?" I asked, willing my voice not to crack.

Dex's fingers tightened. "Because I promise you I will."

You'd think that would be all it would take from a man I trusted enough to marry, but it wasn't. Don't criticize me until you try to live with a dead guy. It's not easy.

Part of me still suspected Dex was an angel and just didn't want to tell me. Truthfully it wouldn't have surprised me to learn that the Universe had a bigger plan for Dex. He's always been the one with the moral compass. His needle points true north. Mine spins. At that moment, I couldn't have landed on north to save my life.

"You said the same thing to me the night you died."

Yes, that was a low blow, but it was an honest one.

Dex stepped back and for a panicked heartbeat, I thought he was going to walk away. Instead, he pulled out the chair closest to mine and sat down, reaching for my hands.

When our fingers intertwined, he said, "Selby, I can't die again."

Tears filled my eyes, which only made my protective, angry shell harden all the more. "You watched me for five years. *Five* goddamn *years*, Dex. I would have sold my soul for one minute with you, and you did nothing. Now you're back and you want me to trust you never to leave me again? Sorry, but that's one hell of a hard sell."

My words hurt him, but that didn't stop me. He owed me an answer.

"What you just said is the very reason I didn't let you know I was here."

"What are you talking about?"

"You would have sold your soul to see me. A soul isn't something you barter with, baby, but you would have auctioned yours off to the lowest bidder if seeing me was the prize. If I'd given you even one minute, what would you have done to get more?"

I pulled my hands away and banged them hard against the table. "Anything and you fucking well know it. So what?"

"So, I couldn't let you do that."

Unable to sit still any longer, I shoved my chair back and stalked toward the sink, my hands balled into fists by my side before I turned toward him again. "You've got some goddamn nerve pulling that spiritual bullshit on me."

Anger flickered in his eyes. "It's not spiritual bullshit, Selby, it's the truth. You think I didn't want that minute, too? You think I liked watching you go into those hotel rooms when you couldn't stand being alone one minute longer?"

That was sure as *hell* not the card he should have played. "Don't you dare throw that up in my face."

A frustrated rumble rose from his throat.

"I didn't care about the damned hotel rooms, Selby," he said, "I cared what you did to yourself *after*. I cared that you thought you were being unfaithful to a dead man. I wanted you to live, not spend the rest of your life waiting for me."

"Well, that's too damned bad because I did wait and now you're here and we're fucking blowing it because you won't talk to me."

He started to speak, but I silenced him with an angry slash of my hand. I had more to say and he was by God going to listen.

"You think I don't see your eyes when you come home, you son of a bitch? I'm your *wife*. I *know* you, Dex Jensen. I can see when you've gone out there and won some kind of victory and I can see it when whatever the hell you've been doing has gone south. Goddamnit, Dex, *tell me*. I don't just want you here, I want to be a part of your life."

"It's not that easy."

The flat acquiescence in the statement hit me like a two by four. "It's not that *easy*?" I said incredulously. "I don't give a shit about *easy*. How the hell many times have you told me we either pull together or we'll get pulled apart? Jesus, Dex, do you even still love me?"

The instant the words were out of my mouth, I regretted them.

"If you don't know the answer to that," he said quietly, "then we've got bigger problems than me not telling you what I did at the office today."

His statement sucked all the air out of the room. I stood there with my heart in my throat, the cold shame of having gone way too far turning my knees to jelly.

Dex looked at me. He didn't blink. He waited.

Slow minutes passed.

Finally, I said, "You have an office?"

To my immense relief, he let out with a deep belly laugh.

"Christ," he said, holding out his hand. "Come here."

I went, letting him pull me onto his lap, and burying my face against his neck as he wrapped his arms around me.

"You are such a pain in my ass," he said, brushing a kiss against my temple.

"Don't keep me in the dark, Dex. Do whatever you have to do but figure out how to get me back in the loop — and don't you lie to me because I'll know."

He laughed again. "I wouldn't dare," he said. "I can't make a lot of promises, but I won't leave in the night again without telling you."

It wasn't everything I wanted, but it was a start.

When I went downstairs the next morning, I found a beautiful breakfast buffet laid out on the conference table. If having a houseguest meant waking up to this kind of spread, maybe we should take in stray clients more often.

Piling my plate with scrambled eggs, hashbrowns, and more bacon than my arteries needed, I sat down at the table across from Ruth as Olivia appeared in the doorway.

Ernest instantly took it upon himself to be the welcoming committee, no doubt as an apology for making the woman pass out cold the night before.

"Good morning!" he said, drifting toward her. "May I show you to your table?"

Thankfully, Olivia seemed fully recovered and actually giggled when Ernest let out with a few welcoming sparks before morphing into the form of a well-dressed *maître d'hôtel.*

"Do you do that all day?" she asked.

"Do what?" Ernest replied.

"Change into different shapes."

"I do," he said. "Watch this."

Throwing on extra swirling tendrils for dramatic effect, Ernest went into his classic Bogart, complete with fedora, trench coat, and lit cigarette.

"Here's looking at you, kid," he said, nailing the voice.

Olivia all but clapped her hands in delight. When he wants to, Ernest knows how to turn on the charm.

"How do you make the end of the cigarette glow?" she asked curiously.

"That's the wildfire part," Ernest explained, floating beside her as she claimed a plate and loaded it with pancakes before joining us at the table.

After we exchanged greetings, Ruth said approvingly, "You sound much better this morning."

"Thank you," Olivia said as she reached for the butter. "I feel better. I slept more last night than I have in weeks. I must feel safe here because I didn't have any of those horrible dreams. It was wonderful."

We kept the conversation light until everyone filtered in, then we cleared the dishes and got down to business. Ruth put a pitcher of cold water and a tray of glasses in the center of the table. Before the afternoon ended that pitcher would be refilled multiple times. Stressful conversations do that to people. The tension sucks your body dry like a hot desert wind.

Olivia opened with a somewhat delicate "mechanical" question. "How can a vampire and a human woman produce a child?"

Johnny, who can be the king of sexual innuendo when we're verbally sparring, actually looked uncomfortable.

"It would not be chivalrous of me to delve into the details," he said somewhat stiffly. "Let us say the children are produced in the typical fashion."

Oh, hell no. He was not getting off that light.

"Chivalrous or not," I said, enjoying his discomfiture enormously, "some of us require the details. I know how a new vampire is made. The sire drains the human to the point of death and then has the human drink their blood to start the transition. Explain how the dhampir thing works. Exactly."

Johnny shot me a murderous glare, which I met with an expression of complete fake innocence. The vampire fidgeted in his chair, fumbling for a reply, obviously not anxious to play Supernatural Sex Ed teacher with Olivia.

Ruth finally took pity on him. "A vampire must feed before he can be with a woman sexually," she explained.

Okay, I confess, I knew that, but watching Johnny squirm was too much fun.

Still looking phenomenally uncomfortable, Johnny said, "Only at such times can a male vampire in theory sire a child. It is a matter of correct body temperature. In the majority of cases, however, given our extreme age, even the energy derived from a fresh meal will not . . . will not . . ."

"Get the little soldiers marching?" I supplied helpfully.

This time he muttered a French word I did know, "*Merde!*"

Olivia saved him — or possibly herself — from further technical explanations. "You're saying my real parents were a vampire and a human?" she asked.

"Your 'real' parents?" Ruth said.

The woman nodded. "I'm adopted. When my health started to get worse, I began to research my birth family looking for clues about genetic problems. All I found were more mysteries. Now I think I understand why."

"Okay," I said. "You need to start from the beginning."

11

Olivia told a hell of a story. She opened by introducing us to Loser Dad — Vincent Curtis Owen also known as "Vinnie."

"When I started my research, I didn't know much about him," she said. "I had his birth and death dates and a vague idea where he went after he abandoned us when I was six years old."

"Us" being four children: two girls and two boys. Olivia was the oldest. The last time she saw her siblings was when they were being taken out of the courtroom and sent to different foster homes.

Her last clear memory of Vinnie was his silhouette in the door on his way out of her life. For years, she convinced herself he got in his car, drove to the end of the street, and died when a delivery van t-boned his Ford.

It wasn't until she obtained a copy of the child services report that Olivia realized Vinnie didn't die that day. The fake memory may not even represent the day he "left" for good.

Vinnie "left" a lot.

A child's mind can go to great lengths to protect itself. Little Olivia constructed a narrative she could accept and understand.

A dead father hasn't callously abandoned his children. He's fallen victim to fate.

That gave her all the room she needed to blame what happened next on her mother who was, without a doubt, a weak soul, incapable of dealing with four children and a deadbeat husband.

But the truth behind Olivia's fiction of memory ran deeper, and therein lies the greater sadness. She loved the jerk and he appears to have loved her.

Olivia said she had a PDF of the child services report on her phone. After Johnny gave her the wifi password, she emailed the file to him. He printed a copy for each of us.

Even translated through modern technology, we examined a vintage document created on a series of government-issue typewriters. The rows of letters hopped up and down with the uneven striking of the overworked keys, a "j" taking a dive here while a "y" shot up half a line there.

The antiquated nature of the report only made it more poignant.

One sentence seared itself into my memory.

"Mother reports father was extremely good to his first child, but cruel to the other three."

Holy hell.

Johnny wheeled the whiteboard closer to the table and began to construct a timeline as the rest of us attempted to decipher the fragmented contents of the document.

- father Vincent Curtis Owen
- born 1952 outside Washington, D.C.
- served in Vietnam as an M.P., 1970-1972
- no record of his activities 1972-1979, possible first marriage?
- met Madeline "Maddie" Gallo in 1979

- married her one week later
- first child, Olivia Ann Owen born 1980
- three more children in rapid succession
- Vinnie, brush with the law, 1985, stole money from cash register
- abandoned wife and family 1986
- 1987 Maddie gives the children up for adoption
- younger children adopted first
- 1989, Olivia adopted

Honest to God those kids didn't have a chance with Vinnie and Maddie, but to be fair to the mother, nothing in the report suggested she'd had an easy life either.

There were numerous references to her controlling and domineering mother, and even a suggestion that the old bitch moved her lover into the house with her husband right in the next room.

Maddie told the social worker that her father was a weak-willed man. You think?

That section of the report detailed Maddie's rumination over the responsibility she held for the breakup of her marriage. She seemed to blame herself for not "making her husband behave" and expressed regret that she wasn't more like her mother.

That's classic Stockholm Syndrome if I've ever seen it. Identifying with your captors and even cooperating with the abuse they dealt out.

Try as they would, the social workers couldn't talk Maddie into taking her children back, and, at least in Olivia's case that was a good thing.

Vinnie hadn't been much of a bread winner. The thing with the cash register happened at a shoe store. Vinnie cleaned out the till on a Friday night and disappeared for a week. When he was caught and arrested, his mother paid the store back and came up with bail money.

Ah, yes, *Grandmama*.

For a few months after Vinnie disappeared, Maddie and the kids lived with his mother in Maryland. Old Lady Owen, however, sent them back to Massachusetts, ostensibly to live with Old Lady Gallo.

Considering that the social worker discovered Old Lady Gallo charged her daughter $10 an hour to watch the grandchildren, Maddie didn't get much help from Mommie Dearest.

Why the Owens didn't do more to help their daughter-in-law and grandchildren was one of the many questions Johnny inked on a second whiteboard in his neat, ornate handwriting.

Olivia was old enough at the time to remember some details from those few months in between Vinnie's disappearance and the children's abandonment.

She had no memory of being at the Owen house, but she did recall living above a grocery store and being sent downstairs to beg for food.

Maddie also had a series of men in and out of the apartment. Olivia walked in on her mother and one of those boyfriends and got slammed up against a wall for the mistake.

When Maddie did try to go out and work, she left her children with a neighbor who wouldn't let them play outside. Instead, she forced the kids to sit lined up along a wall and would backhand them if they made a sound.

It didn't take long for Maddie to fall apart completely and decide she couldn't take care of the children.

"Take care of" being a relative phrase.

"One day she took us to an official-looking building," Olivia said. "I thought it might have been a doctor's office, which didn't make sense to me because none of us were sick. After a few minutes she told me she was going outside to get her coat. I never saw her again."

The abandonment hit Olivia hard according to the report. She cried non-stop and wandered the orphanage halls in a near catatonic state. The younger siblings were adopted out fairly quickly. Olivia stayed there until age nine, but then she hit the jackpot.

Her folks sounded like wonderful people, agreeing to raise her as an only child at the recommendation of the social workers, but welcoming her into a large and warm extended family.

They cherished Olivia and provided her with every opportunity imaginable.

Now both of her parents were gone. Olivia had a failed marriage behind her. She'd never been able to carry a pregnancy to term, suffering multiple miscarriages.

When she spoke of those children who never were, tears filled Olivia's eyes, but the salty drops didn't fall. I know what it took to hold grief like that in check. It hurts like hell.

I was beginning to develop a healthy respect for the fine fiber of steel running beneath the apparently fragile surface of this woman.

One of the social workers made a prophetic observation back in 1986. "Olivia is a child who has become too used to change."

As an adult, Olivia still accommodated change, but assaulted by a rolling wave of health problems over the past 18 months, the pressure began to take its toll, which is what led her to use her last dime to get to us in San Antonio.

When we'd wrung every possible detail from the report, Olivia said, "I've used what I did know about Vinnie and Maddie to try to find out more about my family on AncestorSearch. Would you like to see the family tree I've put together?"

Johnny already had his laptop open before she finished

asking the question. She logged into her account and pulled up the genealogical table, which Johnny projected on the big flat screen.

We understood enough about her family already to interpret what we were seeing. Olivia knew her paternal grandparents' names were David and Justine Owen. Since we were primarily interested in the paternal line, Olivia steered us in that direction. She had another reason for doing so, but I didn't find out why until later.

Thanks to work already done by a distant maternal cousin who didn't even know Olivia existed, but who was also an AncestorSearch member, Olivia said she had lots of data on Justine's people. David, however, appeared to be a total dead end, which piqued her curiosity and ours.

"I haven't been able to find anything about my paternal grandfather after he left Wrightsville, Georgia in 1941 to join the army," Olivia said. "Given what we now know that seems like a red flag, doesn't it?"

Johnny sat forward in his chair. "It does," he said, eyes keen with interest. "There is no information at all?"

"Nothing," Olivia confirmed. "His draft card says he was born in 1923, but I haven't been able to locate a birth certificate. I have no idea who his parents were."

"Do you have a copy of his enlistment record?" Johnny asked.

Olivia punched a few keys on the laptop, accessing something AncestorSearch called a "shoebox." A printed government form that had been filled out in pencil appeared on the screen.

Whoever took down the information hadn't done well in penmanship class. We were able to make out that David worked as a farmer and listed a "W.F. Owen" as his employer.

"W.F. isn't his father?" Ruth asked.

Olivia shook her head. "I'm not even sure that's an "F,'" she said, "but it doesn't really matter. I've searched the records for W.F., W.H., and W.A. without finding a single match. It's like these people never existed."

Ruth caught the detail we'd all missed — including Olivia who had stared at the enlistment record a thousand times.

"Who was David's first wife?"

"Excuse me?" Olivia said.

"His first wife," Ruth repeated. "There, on the line for next of kin. It says 'wife.'"

Olivia looked like someone had slapped her. "He married Justine right at the end of the war," she said. "Her people were all from Maryland. Maybe it's a mistake."

"Or maybe the apple doesn't fall far from the tree," I said. "It looks to me like David was married when he went into the army. Maybe he abandoned his first wife the same way Vinnie abandoned Maddie."

I had offered up a good working theory, but I also opened a can of worms — one that would crawl all over Olivia's family tree before we were done.

12

The mystery of a Georgia farm boy who went to war wasn't the only unanswered question at the end of that first day. For all his knowledge of vampire culture and theories about the significance of dhampirism, Johnny couldn't explain why Olivia's true nature hadn't become evident until she was 35 years old.

He felt we needed to confer with Don Eugenio immediately, and I agreed. As soon as the sun dipped below the horizon, Johnny and I started to head out.

"You coming with us?" I asked Dex, who was sitting at the conference table with Ruth and Olivia looking at Ancestor-Search documents.

"No," he said, standing up, "but I am going out. I'll probably be back before you guys are done at Eugenio's."

Arching an eyebrow in his direction, I said, "Nice of you to let me know."

"No problem," he said lightly as we approached the stairwell. "I'm looking forward to hearing what the Don has to say."

If Dex could make an effort, so could I.

Catching hold of the sleeve of his jacket, I pulled him into a kiss. "See you when you get back."

Dex returned the kiss with more enthusiasm than I had intended. Thankfully, Johnny never slowed his step, disappearing down the stairs toward the garage as if he hadn't seen a thing.

When Dex let me come up for air, I said, "You're in a good mood today."

Grinning, he said, "Any day when you're not mad at me is a good day."

"You poor, mistreated thing," I deadpanned. "How do you stand me?"

"There are benefits that offset the trouble," he said, with a wicked gleam in his eye.

In spite of myself, I laughed. "Go," I ordered. "You know how testy vampires get when they have to wait."

Johnny might not have been "testy" per se when I reached the garage, but he was standing with his arms crossed leaning against the front fender of the Jeep Grand Cherokee.

"Not a chance," I said, "I'm in a mood to drive a real car."

My daily ride, a sexy 1969 black Mustang, purrs like a Bengal tiger on the open road. I love the deep throated growl of the engine and the sheer power vibrating up through the floorboards, but Johnny was having none of it. He insisted on the Jeep.

When I demanded to know why, the vampire said, "You drive like a maniac in the Mustang."

"What the hell are you worried about?" I said. "It's not like I can kill you."

Johnny refused to budge. "I do not wish to be the first vampire in the history of our kind to suffer a major coronary incident. The Jeep, *s'il vous plaît*."

"Fine, Grandma," I grumbled. "We'll take the Jeep."

Don Eugenio lives in a gracious hacienda outside what he calls the "bothersome modernity" of the city. Hints of Mediterranean architecture are evident in the white stucco building with its red terra cotta roof. A rounded turret crowns the entrance and splashes of blue and yellow tiles harken to the days of the Moorish occupation of Spain.

I'm reasonably sure the Don was alive then, by the way. He appears to have been turned in his late 30s, which would put his date of birth around 977 — not quite 200 years after an African army under Tariq ibn-Ziyad invaded the Iberian Peninsula.

The Don has never told me who sired him or who he was before he became a vampire. Whether it's a consequence of birth or careful cultivation, however, Don Eugenio Seguín bears the mark of nobility.

When Johnny and I arrived, the Don's day butler was still on duty. He escorted us through the home's central courtyard past the sparkling fountain to the door of the study where Eugenio greeted us with swashbuckling élan.

Dressed in a white silk shirt open at the neck and black trousers tucked into gleaming equestrian boots, the Don cut a rakish figure straight out of some old movie.

The fact that he held a fencing foil in one hand completed the picture. Eugenio possesses near legendary skills with a blade, talents I know were not cultivated in the name of sport.

When he saw me, the Don's face broke into a broad smile that made the ends of his thin, black mustache twitch. Even with the pallor that comes from centuries of never seeing the sun, Eugenio manages to give the impression of swarthiness.

Tossing the foil to one of his bodyguards, the Don wrapped me in a wonderful, bone-crushing hug. It was about 98 degrees that day, but the vampire's icy embrace felt like diving into a blast of air conditioning.

"Selby, *mi niña hermosa*," he said. "What intricate problem do you bring to my doorstep this fine day?"

Laughing against his shoulder, I said, "You're going to have to sit down for this one."

"Then sit we shall," he said, releasing me and greeting Johnny with a continental *la bise*, one manly kiss per cheek followed by a stout clasping of forearms and a burst of French I guessed was a good-natured insult since both men laughed.

We followed Eugenio to the room's sitting area where he served me a tall glass of iced tea before offering Johnny something darker and redder in a wine glass.

"I understand you have been reunited with your husband," the Don said, "*por la gracia de la Virgen María.*"

It didn't surprise me that Eugenio knew about our last case. He knows everything that happens in his territory. I should have let it go, but if there's a rattlesnake for the poking, you can always count on me to wade in.

"Do *not* tell me you let that asshole Shadow Man get away with what he was doing for centuries," I said.

Nobody, and I mean nobody speaks to Don Eugenio that way except me. The old vampire likes that I'm not afraid of him. We have a policy of total candor between us.

"Of course, I did not," the Don said. "I knew only that an ancient power resided deep in the rocks beneath the school. It did not trouble me, so I did not trouble it. Had I known children were being harmed, that state of *détente* would not have existed."

That's what I expected him to say, but supernatural politics can make for strange casket fellows. Better to check.

"Fair enough," I said. "Do I need to tell you we have a visitor from Massachusetts staying with us?"

The Don laughed. "You give me much greater credit for

micromanaging my holdings than I deserve. Is this guest from the northeast of interest to me?"

"She will be when Johnny tells you about her blood tests," I said.

While the two vampires talked, I leaned against the deeply tufted cushions of the leather couch and listened. Thankfully I knew the details because the two men have a bad habit of drifting in and out of French and Castilian Spanish.

The first time Johnny said "dhampir," Don Eugenio responded with a word that jumped straight across the language barrier: "*herejía*" — heresy.

"Have you ever encountered a dhampir in your lifetime?" Johnny asked.

Eugenio's eyes darkened. "Only once, centuries ago in Spain. He was a creature caught between worlds, a pawn to self-serving humans and vampires alike. The creation of a dhampir is a serious transgression punishable by death."

Without thinking, my hand went to the butt of my pistol. "That's not happening," I said quietly.

"*Por los santos,*" Eugenio said impatiently. "I do not speak of this Olivia Reynolds. She did not ask to be born. She now resides on my lands and is therefore my responsibility and entitled to my protection. Punishment must be meted out to the vampire responsible for this abomination. We will help the girl. Of that, there is no question."

Murmuring an apology, I eased away from my weapon, uncomfortable under the Don's penetrating gaze. "*Qué está mal, pequeña?*" he asked me. "Why would you reach for your weapon under my roof?"

"I'm tired," I lied. "My bad."

Lying to any vampire is hard. Lying to one as old as Don Eugenio is impossible.

"Johnny, *mi amigo*," Eugenio said amiably. "I would like a few minutes alone to confer with Selby."

"*Mais bien sûr*," Johnny said, rising to his feet. "May I avail myself of your library?"

"Please," the Don said, "spend as much time among my books as you like."

"Did it occur to either one of you to ask if I wanted to be 'conferred' with?" I asked sourly.

Two equally perplexed sets of vampire eyes fixed on me as both men said at the same time "*non*" and "*no*."

So much for immortal gender enlightenment.

Johnny exited, closing the heavy plank door behind him. Several seconds of silence passed before Don Eugenio said, "When did the episodes begin again?"

The question ignited firing flashes of memory. A bird screaming in the night. Hooked talons slicing the air. Moonlit golden eyes — and the iron grip of cold arms holding me back. The recollection of Eugenio's long-ago voice echoed in my mind:

"You cannot save him, hija."

That was the night Don Eugenio Seguín saved my life and changed its forward momentum forever.

The vampire must have heard my heart rate quicken.

"*Perdóname*, my friend," he said gently, "but if you do not tell me, I cannot help."

There was no point in denying what he already knew. "Right after Dex reappeared," I said.

"Is this an effect of your struggle with the Shadow Man or a consequence of having been in the presence of *La Santa Madre*?"

"I don't know."

"Have you endeavored to find out?"

"No," I said stubbornly. "I can control it."

Eugenio looked at me with that same immobile patience I get from Johnny all the time. Vampires don't have to breathe — or blink.

"What?" I asked defensively.

"If you could control the curse of *La Lechuza*," Don Eugenio said, "I would not see her violet fire in the depths of your eyes."

"Don't call her that," I said defensively, as more voices from the past rose in my memory.

"My God, Liz, what have you done?" my father whispered hoarsely.

"I've gotten real power," she hissed. "You can keep playing the establishment's game, but I'm done. We've been here for more than 16 years and we've barely made a dent! There are people in this town who need justice."

His next words quivered with outrage. "Of course, they need justice, but you're talking about turning yourself into some kind of vigilante. You can't seriously believe this bruja *can give you that kind of power?"*

Bruja. The Spanish word for witch.

"Are my eyes that obvious?" I asked Eugenio, fear rising to edge the words.

"I do not believe so," he said soothingly, getting up to open a crystal decanter of whisky. He poured three fingers in a glass and handed the drink to me.

"Thanks," I said, taking a healthy slug of the Scotch.

Eugenio filled a second glass for himself and sat across from me in one of the wing chairs by the cold, baronial fireplace. "You have become close with the Acadian witch, have you not?" he asked.

I nodded. "Yes," I said. "Ruth has already guessed what's going on with me. I've promised to come clean with her about everything, but we haven't talked yet."

"Do not delay the conversation for long," the Don advised. "Your souls have traveled together in the past. The witch will comprehend the bargain La Lechuza struck and the damage she caused."

La Lechuza. The Owl Witch. Also known as "Mom."

"One thing at a time," I said, taking another hit of the amber liquid. "First, let's tackle this dhampir business, then we'll worry about me."

The Don didn't like my answer, but he changed the topic of conversation without arguing.

"We must discover the identity of *Senorita* Reynold's sire," Eugenio said. "Find out what you can while I make inquiries in the immortal community."

"Deal," I said, downing the remaining whisky and standing to leave.

Eugenio was on his feet and beside me before I even swallowed.

"Do not neglect your well-being, *pequeña*. I will not allow it. Remember, I was there the night her talons struck your flesh."

I almost said, "yes, sir," but caught myself, answering instead with a curt nod before the Don embraced me again.

"Your father was taken from you most cruelly," he whispered against my ear, "but do not think you are without the love and protection of a *patrón*."

Don't sell the monsters short. Some of them are better humans than the rest of us.

13

"You're back mighty quick, Dexter," Thaddeus said, opening the cabin's rusty screen door. "You left ten minutes ago."

"Here, maybe," Dex said, "but there it's been almost three days."

The old cowboy crossed the weathered floorboards and sat down heavily in a rocking chair. "Olivia get down from Massachusetts in one piece?" he asked, removing his battered Stetson and wiping his forehead with a red bandana.

"She arrived," Dex said, taking the other rocker, "but I'm not sure I'd say in one piece. I'm never going to complain about having a complicated family again."

Settling his hat back on his brow, Thaddeus said, "How'd the missus take your answer?"

"About like I told you she would," Dex said. "The only word she has for what I am is 'ghost.' She's not ready to know the rest."

Trying to keep a straight face and failing, Thaddeus said, "You could tell her that you're corporeal because the electrical repulsive force of negatively charged electrons makes you appear solid."

"You know, Thad," Dex said, "every now and then you're a real son of a bitch."

DEX STEPPED out of the shimmering nimbus of light on the stairwell to find Ruth Beauchene sitting on the stairs.

"Where do you go when you do that?" she asked.

Dex countered the question with one of his own. "How did you know I'd be returning on this spot?"

The witch laughed, moving over on the step. "I have no intention of playing a game of 'show me yours and I'll show you mine' with a corporeal ghost. Have a seat. There are some things we need to discuss."

Dex lowered himself beside her. "What do you want to talk about?"

"Not what, *who*," Ruth said. "I want to talk about Selby."

Dex frowned. "Did something go wrong at Don Eugenio's?"

"They're not back yet," Ruth said, "but since Helen is camped out with Olivia in front of the TV watching a movie, I'd say no. Helen would know if something was wrong with Selby. Actually, Helen *does* know something is wrong."

"She does?" he asked evasively.

Ruth shifted and put her back against the railing. "Do you remember the day we met, Dex? In the rose garden behind the school?"

"Of course. Why?"

"What did you ask me to do that day?"

"To be Selby's friend with a pulse, which you've done," he replied.

Ruth crossed her arms. "Just so you understand, I would

have been Selby's friend whether you asked me to or not. She's a remarkable woman."

"Where is this conversation going, Ruth?"

Anger flickered in the witch's eyes. "It's one thing for you to hold out the truth about your corporeality," she said, stopping him with a curt wave of her hand when he started to protest. "That's your business, at least for now. What I want to know is when you planned to share with me that your wife suffers from a supernatural infection."

Dex looked stunned. "I didn't tell you about the infection because Selby told me she was cured years ago before we even met. I only know about it because she has claw marks on her shoulder."

"Claws from *what*?"

"I don't know," he admitted. "Selby said she was attacked by something supernatural and was sick for a while. Helen's grandmother cured her. There are three slashes on her right shoulder that start out wide and come together in a point like a triangle. How did you find out? I'd lay money Selby didn't tell you."

"You'd win that bet," Ruth said grimly. "If Olivia hadn't seen Selby's eyes, I wouldn't have suspected anything."

"*Olivia* saw something?"

Ruth shook her head. "Whatever you are now, you certainly didn't get enhanced powers of observation. You were right there in the room when it happened."

"When *what* happened?"

"Olivia saw something in Selby's eyes right before Ernest dropped out of rhododendron mode," Ruth replied. "I confronted Selby about the incident last night. She told me she has the condition under control, but when I insisted, she let me touch her. I felt the power of what she's trying to contain. How can you not have felt it, too?"

Dex looked away. "Selby and I haven't been winning any

communication awards," he said uncomfortably. "How bad is it?"

Ruth sighed. "She mostly told me the truth. For now, she seems able to handle the effects of the poison. If her stress level goes up that will get harder, which you and I also need to discuss. Helen says Selby is upset because you're keeping secrets from her. Is that going to stop?"

He leaned forward, resting his elbows on his knees. "Stopping isn't that simple. There are things I can't tell Selby."

The witch considered his words quietly, and then asked, "Can you tell me?"

Still staring at the floor, Dex weighed the request. Finally, he said, "Some of what I've been doing involves gathering information about the Shadow Man's children."

Ruth's eyes widened. "Please tell me that's not a problem that's about to land on our doorstep. I don't think any of us can cope with half-demon children and dhampirs at the same time."

Dex chuckled, "I think you could handle all that and a hell of a lot more, Ruth, but no. There's no activity on the Shadow Man front so far as I can tell."

"Good," she said. "We have enough on our hands. According to Helen, Selby has been especially on edge because she wakes up and finds you gone in the night. Can you at least stop doing *that*?"

"Yes," he said. "I promised Selby there won't be any more disappearing acts. Should I try to talk to her about her eyes?"

Ruth's expression softened when she heard the painful uncertainty in his voice. She laid a comforting hand on his arm.

"I don't think so," she said. "Selby opened her mind to me. I could sense she doesn't want you to know. She promised to tell me what happened. When she does, I'll try to convince her to talk to you, too."

Dex swallowed, but said nothing, dropping his head rather than meet Ruth's gaze.

"I'll do everything in my power to help her," the witch assured him again. "I promise."

Nodding, Dex said, "Selby still isn't sure I'm not going to disappear again without warning. She's terrified of losing the people she loves. That fear opened the door for whatever this is to come back, I know it did."

Ruth's fingers tightened. "How Selby dealt with her grief isn't your fault. She simply couldn't face living without you."

When Dex raised his head, his eyes were bright with tears. "I know," he said, "but now that I'm back, she doesn't know how to live *with* me either."

ON THE WAY back to the office Johnny asked if I realized Don Eugenio would most likely ask me to kill the vampire who sired the first dhampir in Olivia's family.

Keeping my eyes on the road, I said, "Yeah, I got that part."

"Are you prepared to assume that responsibility?" Johnny said. "After the last time, you used quite colorful language to assert to Eugenio that you are not a hit woman."

Except for those times when I am.

I'd love to be able to run interference between humans and the supernatural world without having to kill anyone or anything. Over the last twenty-four years or so, however, I've hardened myself to the reality that sometimes there's no other way.

Most of the time, I can put a bad guy down and file it away as a necessary expediency. The case Johnny was referring to, however, will haunt me until the day I die.

Staring fixedly at the far reach of the headlights, I said, "Last time he asked me to put down a kid."

"A child turned too early in life to understand the need to control her desires or to understand the danger she presented to humans and vampires alike," Johnny pointed out. "What you did was an act of supreme mercy."

Maybe after he tells me that another couple of hundred times I'll start believing it. Intellectually, I know he's right, but pulling a trigger shouldn't be an intellectual exercise. The day I become dispassionate about killing, I'll know I'm lost.

Until I learned about dhampirs, I thought the most sacred vampiric law was "thou shalt not turn a child." Actually, I still think that should be the first undead commandment.

Every human who has been turned goes through an existential crisis. One day you're Joe Ordinary; the next, you can leap buildings in a single bound and sway people with the power of your mind.

Keeping that shit in check requires ethical adjustments children can't manage. Low impulse control and love of instant gratification overrides any sense of responsibility. We're talking a one-way ticket straight into homicidal madness. Even turning an 18-year-old pushes the envelope.

The vampire I put down for the Don was turned a week after her 12th birthday. I swear to you, I've faced rabid werewolves, hell beasts, and bona fide demons that did not terrify me as much as that kid.

I freed her soul the only way I could, but I still have nightmares about it. In my heart, I knew she was a monster, but staring down the sights of my Glock, I looked straight into the face of a cherub.

Now, killing the sick son of a bitch who turned her? That never cost me one minute's sleep.

"We can't let some power-hungry vamp sire dhampirs until

he creates a race of hybrids," I said. "I'm good with taking the guy out."

The weight of Johnny's gaze forced me to steal a glance toward the passenger seat. The lights from passing cars glinted off his eyes.

"We must be completely accurate in our identification of the guilty party," he said. "When we determine the location of the responsible vampire, Don Eugenio will most certainly expect us to bring him to justice. To facilitate our movements as his emissaries, the Don will negotiate diplomatic passage for us across not only the applicable territories, but also through the lands of individual clans. A mistake on our part could be the spark that ignites a war, especially if we travel through the South. Such a conflict has not happened in this country since the division of the northern and southern vampire clans during the American Civil War."

You have no idea how much I wish Johnny would not spring that kind of thing on me when I'm driving down an interstate highway doing 70 mph.

"I thought the vamps took sides during the Civil War primarily for territorial reasons," I said.

"They did," he said, "but you must realize that with territory came resources."

Resources. He meant slaves as a blood sources.

Just when you think you already understand all the slimy parts of your country's history, somebody turns a rock over and something new and even more disgusting comes crawling out.

I didn't say anything for a couple of miles, while my brain processed the information. Then it hit me. Crap. I'd been thinking about vampires inoculated with a dhampir blood serum who could walk around in daylight manipulating human systems. Johnny was suggesting the potential for the enslavement of the human race by undead overseers who never experienced the weakness of being confined indoors when the sun was up.

Johnny sensed my comprehension. "Now you see," he said quietly. "Even among vampires there are gradations of evil. If the vampire who created Olivia's father or grandfather dates to the Civil War period, he could be contemplating a much broader extension of human slavery."

"All the more reason to take him out."

"Dear Selby, while a single vampire may be responsible for siring a dhampir, I believe we should be thinking in terms of multiple offspring. Olivia does, after all, have siblings, all of who could also be exhibiting vampiric traits."

That's when I almost ran off the road.

My mind flashed back to the moment Olivia talked about her miscarriages. Family mattered to her — mattered in ways the rest of us couldn't understand. If she had siblings, she'd want to protect them. I had no idea how she'd feel about their sire.

What the hell were we going to do if she wanted to protect *him*?

14

When Johnny and I got back, everyone gathered in my office for a run-down of our meeting with the Don. I offered a slightly edited version of the conversation for Olivia's benefit, emphasizing the need to find the vampire in her family tree.

She seemed to like the idea of continuing her genealogical research with our help. At the time we had no way of knowing it would take us most of the next week to find a name to take to Don Eugenio.

Ruth moved into the room next to Olivia's for the duration of the investigation, ostensibly to be there for our client, but I suspected to keep an eye on me as well. I'd never admit it to anyone, but I liked knowing she was in the building.

Of course, there were other things that happened during that week as well. For one, Dex still refused to explain the mystery of his existence to me. I didn't take that well — at all.

He slept on the couch while I did everything but sleep. I will give him this; he didn't leave once during the night nor did he interfere with me when I restlessly roamed the building at all hours.

On Tuesday morning, Helen popped in after Dex left for a run to ask me how long I planned to stay mad at him.

"I haven't decided yet," I said, slathering peanut butter on a piece of toast.

"Is this the hill you want to die for, Selb?" she asked, hovering beside me.

"What's that supposed to mean?"

"He's back," she said. "Lots of wives deal with husbands who can't talk about their work. Would you act like this if he had a government job and a security clearance?"

"Probably," I growled. "And how the hell do you know he has a job?"

She held her hands up in self-defense. "I don't know anything," she said, "but staying mad like this isn't good for you. It makes room for the other thing."

Tossing the knife into the sink with a clatter, I said, "Stop! Just. *Stop*. I don't want to talk about the 'other thing.' Don't you have a mall to haunt?"

Thankfully, I held my temper around Olivia. Working on her family research actually helped. I discovered I liked sifting through old documents online and tracking down leads through census records and tax rolls. Go figure.

Sometime toward the end of the week, I started to go downstairs around 1 a.m. to talk to Johnny about the latest tests he'd run on Olivia. Before I reached my destination, however, Ernest materialized on the stairs in front of me.

"Hey," I said, "what's up?"

A hand appeared out of the cloud of smoke as the elemental held an imaginary finger to his equally imaginary lips. "Follow me," he whispered, sending a tiny cloud of grayish particles in my direction.

Stifling the urge to cough, I said impatiently, "Just tell me."

Ernest didn't answer, instead beckoning me to follow by

crooking a make-believe digit.

Grumbling under my breath, I trailed down the hall behind his undulating form toward my office where a single light burned.

The door stood open revealing Olivia sitting at the head of the conference table. She was staring at the big screen TV, which currently displayed the contents of her family tree projected from an open laptop.

"Every night after you all go to bed she comes back down here," Ernest whispered, his voice nothing but a hint of breath against my ear. "I think this is getting to her more than she's letting on. You should talk to her."

"The touchy-feely stuff is more Ruth's department," I murmured. "Why don't you go get her?"

"Olivia needs to know that you understand her, too," Ernest said. "Up in her room, she's got a worn-out copy of *Texas Monthly*. It falls open to that picture of you looking all bad ass. She came to Texas in the first place because she thinks *you* can help her. So, help her."

Great.

I went into the room.

"Hey," I said by way of greeting. "Can't sleep?"

Olivia looked away from the screen. There were dark circles under her eyes and she'd been crying.

"I had a bad dream," she admitted.

"About what?" I asked, turning one of the chairs around and sitting down with my forearms resting on the curved back.

Wiping tears from her cheeks, Olivia said, "In my dream, I saw my family tree covering the whole side of a building. It was huge, and all the branches were alive. Green leaves kept bursting out and starting new connections."

"That doesn't sound so bad," I said.

"That part wasn't," Olivia said, "until the branches lifted off the wall and reached for me. I tried to run, but the tree roots wrapped around my ankles and held me in place. Then all the limbs converged on me at once, squeezing the air out of my lungs, and breaking my ribs."

"I stand corrected," I said sympathetically. "That part sucks."

"There's more," she said, reaching for a fresh tissue. "The scene changed. The tree was growing on the lawn of a courthouse in that same little town that I always see. I know I've never been there, but it comes back over and over in my dreams."

"Could you see any details about the place?"

She shook her head. "Only that it's someplace rural and hot, unbelievably hot. I could feel the sun bearing down on me. My flesh began to sear and then the branches burst into flames. That's when I woke up, but not before I saw him."

"Saw who?"

"A man on the steps of the building," she said, her voice shaking with the memory. "He stood there staring at me through the flames and then he started to laugh. I could still hear that horrible cackling sound in my mind when I woke up."

Take it from someone who knows her way around a nightmare. The last words you want to hear when you finally get out are, "It was just a dream." For the time that you're trapped in that twisted reality, you experience the dreamscape in full living color.

"Is this the first nightmare you've had since you've been here?" I asked.

She nodded. Then, out of nowhere, she asked, "Do you have a lot of family?"

Not the turn of conversation I expected, but I answered her. "Not any more. They're all dead. Dex, Johnny, Ruth, Helen — that talking ashtray, Ernest, they're my family now. Why do you ask?"

Olivia looked longingly at the genealogical chart on the

screen. "I love my adopted family," she said, hot tears spilling from her eyes. "They saved my life, but I always wanted to know about my birth family. I thought — hoped — they might be nice people."

"They could be," I said, but even to my ears it sounded lame.

She looked like she wanted to say something else but couldn't bring herself to speak the words.

"Hey," I said, "you can build any kind of family for yourself that you want. I sure as hell have."

A half-choked laugh escaped Olivia's lips. "That's true," she said, meeting my eyes.

There it was again — a feeling almost like deja vu. What the hell was it about this woman that raised a blip on my radar?

"There's no stopping all this now, is there?" Olivia asked.

Jesus, who the hell could blame her for having cold feet. I wasn't going to insult her by trying to sugar coat a damn thing.

"No," I said. "Even if you decided to throw on the brakes and walk away, Don Eugenio would pursue the case. The implications for dhampir blood in vampire society are too serious to be ignored."

"What have I started?" she asked.

"*You* haven't started anything," I said. "The vampire we're trying to find started it."

"Then why do I have a terrible feeling that whatever this is, I'm going to be the one who has to finish it?"

On impulse, I caught hold of her hand. "This much I can promise you," I said. "You won't have to finish anything alone."

I hadn't meant to make her cry harder, but I did. "Thank you, Selby," she whispered. "You have no idea how much that means to me."

At the edge of my peripheral vision, I saw Ernest giving me a quiet thumbs up from the doorway. Fine. In a pinch, I guess I *can* do the touchy-feely stuff.

15

Getting over the hurdle of David Curtis Owen's life before his enlistment proved to be a bigger obstacle than we imagined. We couldn't find one shred of evidence that the guy even existed before he signed up to join the Army.

At one point even Johnny threw up his hands and let loose with a barrage of French that Ruth translated as, "He wishes we could find a birth certificate."

"Is that *all* he said?" I asked, watching the agitated vampire stalk out of the room.

"I may have left out the more colorful parts," she admitted.

If you don't know where your birth certificate is at the moment? Do your descendants a favor. Go find the damn thing and put it somewhere safe.

That single piece of paper contains a goldmine of facts. Date and place of birth. Name of the parents. Even the name of the doctor can be enough of a lead to fill in an elusive, gaping hole in a family tree.

Normally, we didn't approach an investigation by camping out at the conference table armed with laptops, but Olivia granted everyone on the team access to her AncestorSearch account. We were all working to piece together her family tree, even Ernest, who proved to have an uncanny memory for names, dates, and familial connections.

The third time the elemental explained the difference between a first cousin once removed and a second cousin to me, I almost choked on the soot from his exasperated sigh.

"What is the point of all this goddamned cousin math anyway?" I snarled.

From the doorway, Johnny said, "Because the latest DNA tests have broadened my understanding of Olivia's potential genealogy."

Looking up from her laptop, Olivia said, "Really? How?"

"It is possible that you are the *granddaughter* of a vampire," Johnny said, reclaiming his place at the table. "Perhaps even the great-granddaughter. What dear Selby calls 'cousin math,' could help us determine the accurate connection since we do not have the names of David's parents."

Still behind the rest of the class, I said, "How the hell does that work?"

Beside me, Ernest let out another plume of exasperated smoke, "Selby, come on. Everyone has two parents, four grandparents, eight great-grandparents, sixteen great-great-grandparents . . . "

"I get the idea," I snapped. "What's your point? Olivia's DNA results haven't been loaded onto the site because the service tagged her test as corrupted."

Johnny gave me his most disarming smile.

"What did you do?" I asked suspiciously.

"Merely availed myself of the DNA database by an alternate means of access."

"You *hacked* AncestorSearch?"

"'Hacked' is such an unpleasant word," he shrugged. "The

services tests only a fraction of the potential genetic markers, a mere 700,000. I edited the data I acquired from my tests of Olivia's blood and through an alternate means of ingress, inserted her results into the service's database. We are now free to compare her profile to the others that reside in the servers."

I held up my hand. "Don't tell me anymore. I have to be able to lie convincingly if the Feds show up on our doorstep. Just do it."

He leaned over Olivia's laptop and began tapping keys. The screen split with AncestorSearch on one side and a custom interface on the other. "This program should allow us to more efficiently scan the service for possible DNA matches. When we have located the appropriate common grandparents, we can, perhaps, work back to David Owen's parents."

As hits filled the screen, Ruth joined their efforts while Dex, Helen, Ernest, and I returned to fleshing out the details of how David lived his life. One way or another, we were going to find the odd man out at the family reunion — the one with pointed dental work and a thing for platelets.

David definitely did not lead an uncomplicated life. First, we discovered he had another wife in between the Georgia girl he abandoned and Justine, the wife Olivia knew about — who turned out to be the third wife.

Confused? So were we.

The second wife, Agnes Goldstone, worked as a nurse at Bethesda Naval Hospital where David was stationed as a medic. They were only married a couple of years. If we were right, Justine was pregnant when she and David married. She was also 17 years old.

He and Justine stayed in the Washington, D.C. area after the war where David worked as a cab driver. The city directories, census records, and high school yearbooks available online suggested David and Justine raised a conventional family until Vinnie, Olivia's father, came along.

Young Mr. Owen got himself arrested for the first time at age sixteen: forgery. Vinnie took his mother's checkbook and had himself a high old time in our nation's capital.

I'm not sure why he felt the need to steal her checks since Justine seems to have spent money on him frequently, willingly, and generously. Vinnie was a Mama's boy and a damned spoiled one at that.

But before we get to the storied and sordid career of Vinnie Owen, let's get back to his father, David. We already knew there were plenty of people named Owen in the county, but we couldn't connect them until Olivia, Ruth, and Johnny came up with a potential fourth cousin and a second cousin.

Don't ask me to explain how they did it, but those two DNA matches led them to a common great-something-or-other grandfather and then they started eliminating siblings and matching up family names. The whole thing gave me a headache until The Judge cropped up.

His Honor George Washington Owen — whose child was born and died in the same month in 1923.

The same month David's enlistment papers recorded his birthday.

The Judge's child, however, did not appear to have been given a name, nor were there any graves in the family cemetery for an unnamed infant.

Johnny, who had been mapping out the cousin/grandparent connections on one of the whiteboards said, "We do not have a place in the tree for this Judge. He, like David, does not seem to have left an official paper trail."

Helen was the one who figured out why.

She was hovering behind me staring at a 1920 census roll enumerating the members of the Owen household.

"Who's Cora Herbert?" she asked.

Bleary eyed from staring at the computer screen and almost brain dead from listening to Johnny's DNA theories, I said, "Probably the next-door neighbor."

"No," Helen said stubbornly, "she's not. She lists the same address as the Judge. Scroll to the right."

Helen can read a computer screen, but she can't manipulate one; I scrolled.

"Aha!" Helen said. "Look! Cora is listed as a 'boarder' in the Judge's household."

"And?" I asked.

Ruth joined us. She stared at the handwritten entries, then called up the 1930 census. Cora Herbert was still listed as a boarder in the judge's home.

My mind woke up and headed straight for the gutter.

"Are you thinking what I'm thinking?" I asked Ruth.

She nodded. "In those small Southern towns the county judge was not a man whose behavior would be questioned. Perhaps Cora was there for His Honor's personal pleasure."

"And that baby boy who was born in 1923 didn't die," I said. "Maybe he was given away because he was illegitimate."

Johnny was now looking at the screen as well. "Perhaps he was *illegitimate* in a most unusual way," he said. "If the sire of Olivia's dhampiric line was George Washington Owen, he would have gone to great lengths to disguise the birth of his son and to hide him from detection."

"Hide him?" Ruth asked. "Why?"

"To wait and see what the boy would become," Johnny said. "If Olivia's emerging abilities remained dormant into adulthood, perhaps that was also true of David. His usefulness might not have been immediately apparent."

Olivia, who had quietly called up back issues of the

Wrightsville newspaper while we talked, said, "Guys, look at this."

There were two browser windows open on her laptop. One held a photo of Judge George Washington Owen taken in 1925. The other showed the image of "Judge G. W. Owen, III" from 1965.

The hair and clothes were different, but we were looking at the same man. If "our" Judge Owen had been alive in 1965, he would have been 85 years old.

Then Olivia opened a third window. Same newspaper. This time from 2010. The story heralded the unopposed election of "Judge George W. Owen."

"*Reflecting a tradition of service to the people of Wrightsville predating the Civil War,*" the reporter wrote, "*The Honorable George W. Owen remains on the bench where he will continue to protect the best interests of the people of this county.*"

- George Washington Owen
- G. W. Owen
- George W. Owen

The same man living three different lives. We had a vampire to take to Don Eugenio.

FOR THE RECORD, there was more going on that week than a big, long meeting of the Selby Jensen Genealogy and DNA Club. I had a lot to think about, so I alternated between keeping my mind on the case and burning through ammo on Luther's gun range.

So much ammo, the guy asked me if there was anything I needed to talk about.

"I just paid you $500 for a set of custom-molded grips," I said. "Get your fricking hand out of my pocketbook."

Luther tugged uncomfortably at his *Cabela's* gimme cap and shifted his chewing tobacco to the other cheek.

"Shit, Selby," he said, "do you always have to be a hard ass? I was asking if something's bothering you and offering to help if I can."

He might as well have poleaxed me. "Hell, Luther," I stammered, "I'm sorry. That's . . . well, that's nice of you. I'm okay. Just a lot going on at the office."

Pausing to aim a stream of tobacco juice at the spittoon at the base of his workbench, Luther said, "You dropped the hammer on 500 rounds today."

"Did I?"

"You did. You also asked me to make you six boxes of silver loads with crosses notched in the top. You're starting to sound like a woman getting ready to go to war. I'm hoping it's not with Don Eugenio."

Sometimes I forget that Luther didn't come by his unusual reloading skills without experiences to back-up his custom-designed ammunition. He had loyalties of his own to consider.

"The Don knows what I'm doing," I assured him. "There's not going to be a war in his territory."

"But there's going to be one somewhere, isn't there?"

All I could say was "maybe," but that conversation was on my mind when I dialed Don Eugenio's private number and said, "We think we know who you should be looking at."

"What is the name?"

I gave it to him.

"Good," the Don said. "Come for dinner this evening. All of you, including Miss Reynolds. I am most anxious to meet her."

16

The instant Helen heard we were going to dinner at Don Eugenio's she informed me she had to take Olivia shopping.

"How are *you* going to take her anywhere?" I asked.

Rolling her eyes, Helen said, "Fine, be a stickler for detail. She doesn't have anything, Selby. A couple of pair of jeans, a blouse or two. She needs stuff."

"The woman has pride, Helen," I said. "What am I supposed to do, hand her a credit card and say, 'go buy yourself whatever you need?'"

"Uh, *no*," Helen said. "I'm going to tell her that part, and we need cash, not a credit card, and the keys to the Mustang."

"Yes on the money, no on the car," I replied firmly. "Call her a cab. The money is in the filing cabinet. Manila envelope. Second drawer, dropped in the back behind all the folders."

"Thanks, honey," Helen said, giving me an air hug. We couldn't touch, but it's the thought that counts.

I didn't know how Helen was going to propose the shopping excursion to Olivia, but I trusted her to make the offer without embarrassing the woman or hurting her feelings.

We'd all gotten fond of our "client" over the last few days and had come to see her as the new kid sister on the team instead of someone who was paying us. Olivia might not know it yet, but I had zero intention of taking money from her.

Since we didn't have to leave for Don Eugenio's for several hours, I decided to run a few errands. To my surprise, Dex was waiting for me in the garage. "Hey," he said. "Mind if I ride shotgun?"

Given the way I'd been treating him for the last few days, he earned serious points for having the guts to suggest getting in the same car with me. Maybe it was time to cut the guy some slack.

"I'll go you one better," I said, tossing him the keys. "You can drive."

"Damn," he said, looking hopeful that his personal tide might be turning, "you never let me drive your baby."

As he held the passenger side door open, I said, "The dying/resurrection thing bought you a few dispensations."

"How many is a few?" he asked, easing his big frame behind the wheel and adjusting the seat.

"I haven't decided yet," I said, settling against the door and allowing myself to enjoy the living, breathing sight of him. "Mind your manners."

"I'll do my best," Dex said. "Look, I thought you should know before we go to Eugenio's tonight that I want to be on the clock for this one."

You have no idea how hard I bit my tongue not to say something sarcastic. Instead I went for a neutral, "Meaning?"

Throwing the car in reverse and backing onto the street, Dex said, "Meaning, I used to be a damned good cop. I'd like to be an active part of what happens next. If I know the Don, he's going to send you looking for this Judge guy. I'm just telling you, I'm onboard."

That did it. The snark could not be contained. "Are you sure we're not talking lightning bolts and flaming swords here?"

Dex grinned but didn't take his eyes off the road. "God, that makes me wish I really was an angel," he said. "That shit sounds like fun."

The banter set a good tone between us. I decided not to mess with it.

After I collected a couple of invoices, which involved threatening to re-invite a bunch of poltergeists back into one deadbeat client's life, Dex asked me if I wanted to take a drive in the country before we went home.

Checking my watch, I saw we had four hours until sunset, so I agreed. Once we were off interstate and on a deserted back road, Dex turned on the Dead and before I knew it, we were doing our time-tested duet to "Uncle John's Band."

Neither one of us can sing for shit, nor did we have the benefit of chemical inspiration like Jerry Garcia and the Deadheads, but it felt normal — like the old us.

When we came to a low water crossing on Cibolo Creek, Dex steered the Mustang under a clump of pecan trees on the side of the road. We got out and walked down to the creek, skipping rocks, and talking.

"Hey," I said, bouncing a flat stone three times off the water's surface. "Can I ask you something?"

"Sure," he said. "What do you want to know?"

"Why haven't you been afraid someone would recognize you since you've been back?"

Dex died in a pretty public way — in the line of duty. The SAPD buried him with full honors. I'll never forget the rows and rows of blue uniformed officers standing at attention when we came out of the church. How the heck were we supposed to explain that Dex was back, and good — or better — than new?

"They don't see what you see," he said, sitting down on a large boulder at the water's edge.

I took a deep breath. "I don't want to fight with you," I said, "but you're going to have to give me more of an explanation than that. We've been dancing around what it means for you to be back ever since that night in the school basement. Don't you think I at least deserve to know whether or not I'm sleeping with a ghost?"

Dex sighed. "You're not going to like the answer."

A tiny sliver of fear snaked up my spine. "What's that supposed to mean?"

"For someone in your line of work," he said, "you don't have a lot of patience with metaphysics."

"Try me."

"I'm alive and I'm not alive."

I groaned, shoving him over and sitting down on the rock beside him.

"You're right," I said, "I can't stand that kind of illogical bullshit. How can you be alive and dead at the same time?"

Throwing me a sidelong glance out of the corner of his Ray-Bans, Dex said, "You did not just say that to me, did you? Your business partner is a vampire. Alive and dead at the same time. Remember?"

Crap. He had me there.

"We're not talking about Johnny," I said irritably. "We're talking about you."

"You identified the body, baby," Dex replied, slipping off his glasses so I could see his eyes. "That werewolf did his job. I died, but I didn't leave. I spent the next five years watching you grieve for me and waiting for you to go on with your life. Then Emily Montrose died in that basement."

Without warning, an image of the murdered girl came into my thoughts. She'd been down there praying to the Virgin Mary to save her from the Shadow Man — with her teddy bear nearby — when she was killed.

"What about Emily?"

"The morning Ruth called you to come to the school, I rode shotgun," Dex said. "You and Rich started to get into it in the hall and I whispered in your ear that he's a good guy."

SAPD Lt. Rich Haversham was Dex's former partner — and a werewolf. Something I didn't find out until the middle of the Montrose case when I erroneously accused Haversham of killing Dex — while I held a gun to the guy's head. Not my finest moment in the judgment department.

Rich and I blamed one another for Dex's death for years and quarreled bitterly any time our paths crossed. I had heard Dex's cautioning voice that morning.

"I remember," I said.

"When you all went down to look at the body, I followed you," Dex continued. "She was there."

"Of course she was there," I frowned. "That's where she was killed."

"Not Emily," Dex said, shifting on the rock. "Her, the Blessed Mother."

My eyes narrowed. "The Virgin Mary *watched* the murder?"

"Not watched," he corrected me, "watched *over*. She stayed at Emily's side."

A lump rose in my throat. "I wish there had been another way for us to stop the Shadow Man. It still tears me up that Emily had to die like that."

"We don't get a lot of say in how the Big Story plays out," Dex agreed sadly. "Anyway, the Blessed Mother sort of showed me another way to be in this world."

"And?"

Dex hesitated, then seemed to come to a decision.

"You know all that stuff you hear about there being a light or a doorway? Well, none of that happened when I died. I woke up in an office. The place looked like something out of an old detective movie from the 1940s. Wood desk. Wire trash basket. A black rotary telephone."

That was not what I expected him to say. "Heaven is a Sam Spade novel?" I asked with a crooked grin.

Dex let out a sharp laugh. "I don't think I was in heaven. More like a waiting room. Anyway, this guy came in. Big dude, busted nose like an old prize fighter, hands all scarred up, dressed like a cowboy out of some Tom Mix movie. He sits down, points to a chair, and says, 'Dexter, let's talk.'"

"You hate it when anybody calls you Dexter."

"I do," he agreed, "but under the circumstances, I figured I better be a good boy and play along."

"What did this guy say to you?"

"He said I had a choice," Dex answered. "That all of existence is about choice."

My throat knotted up again. "So you're here until you choose not to be?"

Dex tentatively put his arm around my waist. When I didn't move away, he pulled me closer.

"No," he said. "That last night in the basement, after I had to watch what the Shadow Man did and said to you, I made another choice. I'm here as long as you need me."

"But what about the identity thing?"

"You see the real me," he said. "The rest of the world sees what I need them to see. I'm whoever I have to be in the moment."

He was right. I didn't like the metaphysical uncertainties of the situation. I damned sure didn't like the secrets, but I did like how it felt to lean into my husband's solid body again.

"We don't have this thing figured out yet," I said, putting my hand over his where it rested against my belly.

"No," he said. "We do not."

"You don't have to sleep on the couch tonight."

I felt him grow still against me. "Just like that? You're good with everything I told you?"

"I'm good with *some* of it," I said. "I'm still pissed as hell about being kept out of the loop, but you're here. Somebody, somewhere, made that happen all neat and tidy. We've got work to do, and I'm tired of fighting with you — for now."

17

Helen and Olivia took an Uber to the mall. In order to bond and share the shopping experience, Helen suggested Olivia slip on a broken Bluetooth headset she knew I'd tossed in the top drawer of my desk. Armed with the tiny device, Olivia could talk to Helen without anyone finding the one-sided conversation unusual.

"It worked *great!*" Helen enthused. "We had such a good time. That girl knows how to shop!"

My ghostly buddy popped in after Dex went downstairs to wait for me to get ready to leave for Don Eugenio's dinner party. No one will ever accuse me of being a clothes horse, but I decided to make an effort to show up in something other than jeans and a black t-shirt since the Don had specified "cocktail attire."

Hovering behind me as I surveyed the contents of my closet — which is filled with jeans and black t-shirts, Helen asked critically, "Do you even own a dress?"

"There's a black one in here somewhere that I wore to Aunt Minnie's funeral," I replied, pushing hangars aside until I found a pair of heather gray pants, "but there's not a chance in hell I'm wearing that."

Tossing the pants on the bed, I continued to riffle through the clothes until I extracted a wine-colored silk blouse.

"I like that," Helen said approvingly. "Why haven't I seen it before?"

Reaching for a pair of nail scissors on the bureau, I clipped off the price tag.

"Oh," she said, "that would be why."

Shrugging out of my t-shirt, I slipped on the blouse. I didn't remember when or why I bought it, but I liked the deep red against my skin. Once I'd replaced my jeans with the dress slacks, I judged myself ready to go. Helen, however, insisted I dig in my jewelry box until I found a flat gold chain and a pair of hoop earrings to replace my perpetual studs.

"Shoes?" Helen asked, hovering cross-legged over the end of the bed.

Giving her the *look*, I asked, "Where exactly do you expect me to put this?"

She stared at the Glock 27 in its ankle holster and said, "Fine, but at least wear the good boots with the low heels. The ones that don't make you look like you're about to join a biker gang."

Making a conscious effort to deflect Helen's critical fashion sense away from me, I said with fake enthusiasm, "What's this about Olivia being a good shopper?"

"Oh. My. *God*," Helen said. "She is the *best*! That woman knows her pocketbooks."

Alarm bells went off in my head.

"How much did that cost me?"

"Not much," Helen hedged.

"Define 'not much.'"

"In between Prada and Louis Vuitton," she said.

I winced. "How, exactly, did a fancy purse become a necessity?"

Helen grew serious. "At first it didn't," she said. "Olivia was super frugal, like in *cheap*. She picked out cute stuff, but nothing extravagant. Then we walked by the pocketbooks and I thought she was going to cry."

By this time, I was brushing my hair. That statement stopped me in mid-stroke. "Who cries over a handbag?"

"Somebody who loves the sheer brilliant artistry of a stylish well-made bag," Helen said with deep and reverent gravity. "Olivia hasn't had a good pocketbook since her marriage broke up. It's been terrible for her."

Not a tragedy I could comprehend, and I said so, "That I don't get. How can not having a good purse be terrible?"

"Okay," Helen said, "imagine this. What if you had to sell all your best guns, the ones you love the most, because you needed the money to pay the bills and all you could afford to carry was a cheap Rossi from a pawn shop."

A shudder ran through my body. "That's like not having a gun at all."

Helen regarded me with a triumphant expression. "Exactly!" she crowed. "A handbag from Sears might as well be a grocery sack."

"This pocketbook thing was Olivia's idea?" I asked.

The guilt on Helen's face was almost funny. "*Well*," she said, "not really. I had to persuade her."

"I'll bet you did," I said, sighing. "Did the fancy bag make her happy?"

Breaking out in a radiant smile, Helen said. "It was a *religious* experience for us both. Olivia is downstairs in her room right now getting ready for tonight and organizing all her stuff in the new bag. She looks as happy as you do every time you come home with a new 9 millimeter."

What the hell? Who am I to judge somebody else's addiction?

Switching topics, I asked, "How does she feel about meeting Don Eugenio?"

Still sitting cross-legged and suspended in mid-air, Helen floated behind me as I walked into the living room. "She's nervous, but excited. I don't think she can imagine anyone who's been alive for a thousand years and I know she has lots of questions."

"Like what?"

"Well, for one thing, Olivia wants to know why in a place as small as Wrightsville no one has figured out that The Judge never gets any older."

I knew what Eugenio would say. Vampires carve out power niches using a combination of mesmerism, fear, and immortal tactics. Every few years, they re-invent their legal identities while throwing a cloak of glamour around themselves that causes the casual observer to see them as older than they appear in their natural state.

Where necessary, some of them are also not above a healthy dose of terror to ensure human compliance. Maybe not the most appetizing dinner conversation, but since at least two people at the table would be sipping a perky Chateau le Neuf Corpuscle, Olivia would need a strong stomach anyway.

We'd finished our conversation on the stairs. From the way Dex's eyes lit up when Helen and I entered the office, I guess I'd done okay with the wardrobe thing. Dex was wearing a black shirt open at the throat, an oatmeal linen blazer, and a pair of dress jeans.

"You look nice," he said. "That color is beautiful on you."

"You don't look so bad yourself," I replied. "Mr. Fussy Fangs should approve of us both."

On cue, Johnny walked in adjusting his gold cufflinks. "*Tout à fait acceptable*," he said, looking us over. "Most refreshing to see the pair of you looking almost cultured."

"That's big of you," I said. "Love the suit."

"You should!" Helen enthused. "That's *Armani*. The tropical wool and silk, right?"

I would have gone with "blue."

"*Oui*," Johnny said. "Do you think the tailor achieved the correct length for the pants? I prefer a clean break over the shoe."

Before he and Helen could lapse into a full-blown fashionista debate, Ruth came through the door in a vintage emerald cocktail dress with a plunging v-neck and a saucy pleated skirt.

If I hadn't been on my best behavior, I'd have told Johnny to wipe the drool off his canines.

Oblivious to the rest of us, he bowed and said something gallant to Ruth in French. How do I know it was gallant? The color rose in her cheeks and she cast her eyes down when she answered him.

Now that she'd read the group, Helen made her own wardrobe choice, shimmering out and back in freshly attired in an upscale take on the classic little black dress.

Ernest chose to go with a Sinatra vibe, right down to the highball glass in one hand and lit cigarette in the other.

"If you break into so much as one verse of '*My Way*,'" I warned him, "I'll hose you down with the nearest fire extinguisher."

The elemental grinned and shifted into a warbling Sinatra imitation that set my teeth on edge.

Before I could tell him exactly how much he'd bitten off, a cough from the door made us all turn. Olivia stood in the doorway dressed in an off-the-shoulder teal summer dress with a pale floral pattern. "Do I look okay?" she asked shyly.

Johnny crossed the room and held out his hand. When

Olivia extended her own, he took it and said, "*Magnifique, mademoiselle. Simplement magnifique.*"

Over my objections, Don Eugenio insisted on sending a limousine for us. The driver stood at attention as he held open the vehicle's opposing rear doors. Two bottles of iced champagne waited for us in the cocooned and heavily tinted luxury of the limo's cabin.

"Not that I'm complaining," Dex said, popping the cork on one of the bottles, "but what's with all the fancy stuff?"

"It is in honor of *Mademoiselle* Olivia," Johnny said. "Eugenio wishes her to see that contrary to popular mythology, vampires are capable of being exceptionally civilized."

Taking her glass of champagne, Olivia said, "It's working. I feel like I've stepped into a fairy tale."

I sipped my champagne and kept my opinions to myself. If Eugenio was going to this much trouble to sugarcoat the medicine? The news about The Judge must be bad. Really, *really* bad.

18

Dinner with a vampire isn't normally that different from dinner with anyone else — unless you're the main course. Since we weren't on the menu, I expected a gracious evening crafted largely for Olivia's benefit.

For the most part, I wasn't wrong.

Don Eugenio met us at the door in a knee-length gilet. The crushed velvet of the gold-embroidered, sleeveless jacket matched the midnight blue of yet another billowing silk shirt. There was no sword this time, but in trim black pants and high-heeled Spanish boots the vampire looked every inch the gentleman pirate.

When I introduced Olivia to the Don, he kissed her hand and said, "*Bienvenido, señorita. Mi casa es su casa.*"

Our Yankee friend surprised me by responding with perfect inflection, "*El gusto es mio.*"

Then things got stranger.

The Don locked eyes with Olivia. If he hadn't still been holding her hand, the dhampir might have backed away. Instead a gasp escaped her lips — a sound more surprised than fearful.

Vampires as old as Don Eugenio keep the psychic volume turned down most of the time. When they don't, I'd tell you to prepare yourself, but it wouldn't help. If you make the mistake of shaking hands or establishing eye contact expect to wake up with complete amnesia about what you've done, said, or donated.

In taking the measure of Olivia with his extrasensory powers, Eugenio didn't have mesmerism on the mind. Without taking so much as a bite, he was tasting her.

His energy crawled over my skin like an army of supercharged ants. Beside me, Ruth cringed as pale static spider webs rippled over her bare forearms. Without prompting, Johnny put out his hand and drew the tiny bolts toward himself.

Later, on the drive home, I would ask Johnny about the Don's impressive display of otherworldly ability.

"I've never seen you do anything like that," I said.

"Don Eugenio is ancient. He can do many things I cannot — many things that few vampires can do."

Even Ernest felt the electrically charged air, hastily dissipating toward the yard where he gathered into an amorphous cloud suspended over a bed of cactus. Lights flashed in his roiling form making the elemental look like a distant thunderstorm waiting to break.

Dex shifted from one foot to the other. "How do we play this?" he murmured.

"We don't," I replied. "We're not in charge."

Don Eugenio controlled the moment — a moment that stretched into eternity before he found out whatever he wanted to know and backed down, replacing the psychic probing with his usual mannerly elegance.

"You are more than I anticipated, *Señorita*," the Don said, bowing again.

Olivia, who had been totally lost in their connection, blinked back to full awareness. "I don't know exactly what you mean," she admitted, "but you're more than I expected, too."

Chuckling, Eugenio offered her his arm. "You will understand in time."

Resting her hand against the smooth fabric of his sleeve, Olivia allowed herself to be escorted into the hacienda. We followed, stepping through a small entrance hall before entering the central courtyard.

An exquisitely appointed round table sat near the gurgling fountain. Oil lamps on the supporting columns provided warm, wavering light without detracting from the breathtaking splash of stars overhead.

"We are well removed from the city here," Eugenio said, pulling out a chair for Olivia, "so we may enjoy the grandeur of the night sky as *El Señor* intended."

A liveried waiter appeared and served wine for the humans. Johnny and Eugenio accepted gold goblets discretely pre-filled to disguise their true contents.

Before joining us at the table, Eugenio turned his attention to Ernest. "My apologies for placing you in close proximity to running water," he said. "Perhaps this will make you more comfortable."

Across the courtyard a second servant ignited a brazier. The heat didn't reach us at the table, but the flames enhanced the sense of temporal displacement I always experience in the Don's home.

The ancient immortal has a way of transporting his guests through time. We could as easily have been in a villa in Andalucia in the 10th century as a hacienda outside San Antonio at the beginning of the 21st.

Ernest eyed the fire and let off a burst of excited sparks. "*Wow!* For me?"

"Entirely for you, my friend," the Don said. "Enjoy."

The elemental shot into the searing depths of the coals sending a column of flame skyward.

"Is that safe?" Olivia whispered to Ruth.

"For Ernest entering a fire is like taking a swim," Ruth assured her. "He's been after Selby to add fireplaces to every room in the building since he moved in with us."

Next, Eugenio and Helen exchanged several bursts of rapid-fire Spanish that were even too fast for me. I *think* mutual compliments about wardrobe were involved.

She would die all over again rather than admit it, but Helen nurses a huge crush for the Don.

With the needs of his non-corporeal guests met, Eugenio pulled back his chair, but remained standing as he raised his goblet.

"A toast," he said gallantly. "To our friend from the north. Welcome to *San Antonio de Béxar*, *Señorita* Reynolds."

Olivia blushed as we lifted our glasses, but I could tell the effusive welcome pleased her.

A casual observer looking into the courtyard that night would have seen six people engaged in an animated and wide-ranging conversation over a superb meal. The two vampires ate nothing, but their abstinence didn't stop the rest of us from enjoying prime rib with all the trimmings.

I noticed Olivia received an exceedingly rare serving of meat. When she didn't hesitate before digging in, I assumed she'd decided to take Johnny's lectures regarding the necessity of high-quality protein to heart.

Eugenio skillfully drew Olivia out of her shell, answering her initial, timid questions with details intended to put the woman at ease and whet her curiosity.

"Why did you decide to come to the New World?" Olivia asked. "I can't imagine what would make me climb into one of those tiny ships and sail off toward the edge of the earth where the monsters lived."

Eugenio looked away, staring into the shadows of memory. In the twilight, his profile looked like the head of a Roman emperor cast in gold.

"When Cristóbal Colón, the man you knew as Christopher Columbus, first reached the Caribbean the *Theatrum Orbis Terrarum* had not yet been printed," the vampire said, the suggestion of a smile lifting the corners of his mustache.

He was referring to the first atlas printed in Antwerp in 1570. The illustrations of mythical creatures that adorned the maps gave rise to the mostly apocryphal phrase "*hic sunt dracones*" — "here be dragons" — to describe the unexplored regions of the known world.

"I had more fear of the religious monsters in the Old World than anything I expected to find in the unknown regions lying beyond the Atlantic Ocean," Eugenio continued. "Ferdinand and Isabella instituted the Holy Office of the Inquisition in 1478."

Johnny moved his chair back and crossed his legs. "I have always considered myself most fortunate to have avoided the Inquisition in France," he said. "The evangelical Protestantism in place during the 19th century when I was turned thankfully did not present the same level of threat."

"Many vampires fled Spain in the years that followed the establishment of the Inquisition," Eugenio said. "I was among them. With the means to finance a small private expedition, I successfully accommodated my unique physical requirements, but only with great difficulty."

Olivia's head swiveled between the two immortals, staring at them with rapt fascination. "What did you do when you got to the Americas?" she asked the Don.

"Avoided murdering fools like Hernan Cortés and Pedro de Alvarado," the Don replied. "If there is a hell, I hope their souls roast there for the crimes they perpetrated against the indigenous peoples. I steadily worked my way north, staying on the edges of colonial society until certain opportunities presented themselves during the founding of San Antonio de Béxar in 1718. I have remained here for almost 300 years."

As the staff cleared our plates, Eugenio suggested the group adjourn to his study "to discuss more modern issues of vampiric politics."

Over snifters of cognac, the Don got straight to business. "Johnny has educated you about the biology of your condition as a dhampir, *Señorita*. Now I have the unfortunate task of introducing you to your great-grandfather."

After I gave Eugenio the name "George Washington Owen" that morning, the Don spoke with the Governor of the Southern Territory of the United States, Malachi Reeves, a thousand-year-old English vampire who migrated to the Carolinas in the 1650s.

Reeves instantly recognized the Judge's name because the two immortals migrated to the Americas together.

"'George Washington' can't be this vampire's true name," Ruth said. "Washington wasn't born until 1732."

Eugenio nodded. "You are correct," he said. "The immortal known today as George Washington Owen was sired in the hills of Scotland almost a millennia ago. There he was known as Seumas Stiùbhart."

"James Stewart?" Ruth said. "Of the Royal House of Stewart?"

"The human branch of the family traces its heritage to Brittany in the 11th century," Don Eugenio said. "They originally were in service to David, King of the Scots and in time married into the royal line. Seumas Stiùbhart became an immortal in 1157 during the reign of King Malcolm IV. When the James

Stewart known to history ascended first the throne of Scotland and then of England, Seumas began to use his middle name Seòras or George in combination with his sire's surname, Owen. I suspect the current appellation of 'Washington' merely amuses him."

King James VI of Scotland and I of England had a nasty hobby — witch hunting. His activities touched off a new round of "monster" immigrants to the New World. Among them the Stewart vampire who called himself George Owen and his sometimes friend, Malachi Reeves.

"Let's skip the history and cut to the chase," I said. "If we're dealing with a thousand-year old vampire, we can't waltz in there and ask him about his love life."

The Don grinned as he took a sip of his Brandy de Jerez. "Ah, but that, Selby is perhaps the most interesting aspect of this story. Although this Judge possesses the age of a master vampire, he does not command the commensurate power, which may well explain his ill-considered decision to sire offspring with a human."

Since he didn't have the chops to play with the big vamps, the Judge apparently decided to create a line of hybrids and use them to make a bid for power in the vampire world. There was one thing Judge Owen didn't count on, however. Not all of those dhampirs would necessarily be willing to play Daddy's game.

Before the coming dawn forced us to return to the office for Johnny's benefit, Don Eugenio gave us quite a lesson in vampire genetics and politics. Seumas Stiùbhart's sire might have made a vampire of a mere mortal, but something went wrong in the supernatural DNA exchange.

According to both Eugenio and Johnny, even immortals can suffer from birth defects. The Judge failed to develop the full range of his powers with the passing centuries. From what

Malachi told the Don, His Honor's abilities roughly equaled those of a vampire of 200 to 300 years.

"George Owen's relative weakness formed the basis of his friendship with Malachi," Eugenio explained. "Malachi protected him from manipulation by stronger immortals in the 16th century and has continued to do so to the present. In recognition of George's great age, Malachi has allowed him to exercise complete control over a small territory in central Georgia surrounding Wrightsville since well before the American Civil War."

Malachi did not, however, know that his old friend had fathered dhampiric children. That crime, one in a long line of excesses on George's part, crossed a line Reeves was not willing to ignore. But, like most master vampires, the Governor preferred to hire out his dirty work.

"You have the Governor's permission to enter his territory and to address this problem," Don Eugenio told me. "Reeves has arranged your safe passage across all territories in the south, but understandably he wishes this issue to be dealt with expeditiously and discreetly."

We'd never come right out and told Olivia that the Judge would have to die for his crimes, nor had we addressed how we'd handle the matter of other dhampirs he'd fathered — mainly because we didn't *know* how we'd work with that last part.

As that night dragged on, however, our client's attention hadn't flagged — far from it. She grew quiet, but only because she was mentally arranging the complex pieces being laid out before her.

From time to time, I'd stolen a glance at Olivia, sitting in one of the big leather chairs by the fireplace. Her small stature coupled with the oversized furniture gave the woman the appearance of a child being allowed to listen to the adults talking late at night, but the light of keen interest and sharp intelligence burned in her eyes.

"You're going to kill him, aren't you?" she finally asked.

Eugenio doesn't believe in pulling punches. "The Judge has broken one of the most sacred laws of our kind. He must die for his crime."

Olivia looked toward me, then back at the vampire. "You're hiring her to do it, aren't you?"

"The Governor has authorized Selby's deputization as an officer of his administration," Eugenio said. "She is empowered by his authority to carry out the death sentence. Do you object?"

Straightening in the chair, Olivia said with both candor and courage, "Are you going to kill me next?"

Ruth started to speak, but Johnny laid a restraining hand on her shoulder. In as gallant a gesture as I have ever witnessed, Eugenio went down on one knee before his guest.

"I have claimed you as a citizen of my territory, Olivia Reynolds," he said. "No harm will befall you, but no mercy can be granted to Seumas Stiùbhart."

With their eyes now on the same level, Olivia said, "Then I ask one favor of my Don."

"Ask," Eugenio said, "and if it is in my power, I will grant it."

"Before George Washington Owen dies, I want him to answer every question I have about my family. I want to know exactly who I am and where I came from, and if there are other dhampirs, I want your word that they will be protected until we find out if they are good or bad people."

"And if they are bad people?" the Don asked.

Olivia answered him with flat resolve. "I will help end them myself."

From the glow in his eyes, that answer pleased Eugenio enormously.

"Upon my word, you will have your answers," he said, looking at me for confirmation.

Nodding, I made my commitment to the deal. "One way or another, the Judge will live long enough to tell Olivia what she needs to know."

"Then it is arranged," the Don said, rising smoothly to his feet. "You will go to Georgia."

19

Even though we'd been up all night, no one felt like sleeping. Back at the office, we changed into comfortable clothes before convening around the conference table. Dex made a quick doughnut run, allowing our planning session to be fueled by equal parts sugar and caffeine.

Snagging a pastry with one hand, I used the other to run a Google search on my phone — "distance San Antonio, Texas to Wrightsville, Georgia."

I squinted at the results. "It's 1,064 miles. Estimated driving time 16 hours and 19 minutes."

"So we fly to Atlanta and rent a car?" Olivia asked.

Our new friend hadn't quite caught up to the technical aspects of life with the undead. "Flying is out," I said. "Too many random factors with a vampire onboard."

Her mouth formed a silent "oh" of comprehension.

Not surprisingly, Johnny and the Don had gotten a jumpstart on the logistics.

"Before we left the hacienda, Eugenio offered the use of his private travel coach," Johnny said. "He provided me with a link to a series of photographs. Shall we review the files to see if the vehicle is acceptable?"

High-definition images snapped into focus on the big screen. We were not looking at any normal person's idea of an RV.

"How much did that thing cost?" I asked, awed by the coach's swank interior.

Johnny sniffed at my lack of manners. "Such a question would have been rude," he said. "Don Eugenio assured me the vehicle possesses the necessary amenities. An immortal of the Don's stature does not allow cost to be a limiting factor in his acquisitions."

The coach's shiny maroon exterior with gold accents and deeply tinted windows gave way to an interior filled with expanses of leather, hardwood, and chrome. Calling up the owner's manual on his tablet, Johnny took particular note of the custom freezer under the floor designed for "extended expedition food storage." Read: mobile blood bank.

Much more than the practical details made the set up perfect for my business partner. The luxury bus screamed money, class, and high-end tech. I could already see Johnny reclining in one of the captain's chairs monitoring fuel consumption with his iPad while contemplating an evening pint of A/B negative by the campfire.

Excuse me. Fire pit. *Portable* fire pit complete with "integrated fire suppression mechanisms for safe disposal of ash and other fuel remnants."

That bit of verbiage came straight from the tech manual and was but one of the many phrases that almost caused the vampire to drool. Phrases like "fingertip controls" and "exquisitely appointed cockpit" rolled off his tongue like whispered endearments to a lover.

On a normal day Johnny nurses an addiction to gadgets — an addiction the coach would allow him to indulge *on wheels.*

I let him drone on until I finished the third doughnut. Then I cleared my throat and said, "Excuse me for being the voice of reason, but is that thing big enough for all of us?"

Honest to God, the vampire looked offended. "The sleeping accommodations are more than adequate for all corporeal members of our happy band," he said. "Surely you cannot imagine Don Eugenio would suggest a mode of travel that would subject the ladies to extended discomfort?"

From the way Johnny gave me the stink eye, I'm not sure he included me in that feminine number — subtle punishment for my critical disapproval of the miraculous vehicle under discussion.

Helen, on the other hand, had no qualms about the coach and was more than enthusiastic about its onboard entertainment options. "Oh, Johnny!" she trilled. "Is that a 50" TV in the lounge?"

"It is," Johnny said, "one that resides in a recessed wall compartment. That section also extends beyond the coach's body to broaden the theater area."

My snark would no longer be contained. "*Theater area?*" I said. "So where's the popcorn machine? Because no popcorn machine is a deal breaker in my book."

Johnny ignored me and continued his conversation with Helen. "The satellite system will ensure, dear Helen, that you do not miss your reality programs and it will provide us with Internet access."

"*Dear Helen,*" I said, affecting a cultured accent. "Would you be so kind as to ask *Monsieur* Devereux if the coach gets one or two blocks per gallon?"

Olivia giggled, and Ruth had to look away, so she wouldn't laugh. Helen remained resolutely on Johnny's side. "Come on Selb, get with the program," she enthused. "We're going on a *road trip!*"

My bestie seemed to have blocked out the memory of our last road trip together — the one where she wound up dead.

Not to be outdone in the self-interest department, Ernest floated into the discussion and morphed into a touristy shape complete with Wayfarer shades and Bermuda shorts.

"I can come, too, right?" he asked nervously. "No fair ditching the elemental."

Johnny made a 'tsking' sound. "We would not dream of leaving you behind," he assured Ernest. "In your amorphous state you are an excellent stealth operative. We will, however, have to disable the smoke detectors when we retrieve the coach tomorrow evening."

That was Ruth's cue. "We need to address scheduling."

Johnny got that look on his face that says, "You're going to ruin this freaking amazing man plan with logic, aren't you?"

Ruth, accurately interpreting his reaction, took the time to soothe the vampire's ego before continuing.

"No one is doubting the magnificence of the coach, Johnny," she said, "but I hope you're not planning for us to leave tomorrow."

The vampire looked completely blank. "Why would we not be able to depart immediately?"

With the same kind of patience I imagined she brought to the classroom, Ruth said, "Johnny, you may be able to throw a few blood bags in the freezer and be ready to go, but travel preparations are more complicated for mere mortals. There are also some logistical aspects I'm not sure you and Don Eugenio have fully considered."

Johnny picked up his iPad and consulted a document, running his finger down the screen. "I cannot imagine what," he said finally.

Smiling at him fondly, Ruth said, "Have either of you ever

been to the kind of campgrounds and RV parks where people park their travel coaches?"

He worked his eyes back and forth trying to determine the relevance of the question.

"Don Eugenio indicated other immortals in his acquaintance use such coaches," Johnny said finally. "He indicated that when he travels to Mexico he does not stop until he reaches land he owns. Is there an issue making use of facilities designed to accommodate recreational vehicles?"

Ruth shook her head. "You're cute when you act your age."

Now she had him flummoxed. "Act my age?"

"As in two hundred plus," I jumped in. "Your big boy toy there may be more expensive than what the average retiree can afford, but people who drive those big RVs are super extroverted. They congregate at campgrounds and parks to *socialize*. You and Eugenio have figured out how we're going to get to Georgia, but you didn't consider how much attention we might attract doing it."

Comprehension dawned. "We will not blend in among other travelers."

"No," I said, "we most certainly will *not*. Don't get me wrong. I'm looking forward to traveling in style as much as you are, but we need to plan a route and work out stops at secluded places — another reason we need more lead time."

Grudgingly acceding to our request, Johnny began to map out minor technological upgrades to the coach. When we compared our goals to his, we settled on a departure time 48 hours in the future.

Next, we put a map on the big screen, deciding to take a straightforward route east out of San Antonio on I-10 to Houston and Beaumont before crossing the border into Louisiana. Then we'd hit Lake Charles, Lafayette, and Baton Rouge.

"How many hours from here to Baton Rouge?" Ruth asked, the place name coming out with Creole inflections.

I consulted the map. "With light traffic, 7 hours and change."

"That's a good first day's drive," she said. "I have connections in Baton Rouge. I'll arrange something for us there and then coordinate with Don Eugenio to make sure we're cleared with the local vampires.

"Okay, good," I said. "That's one night."

"What's the rest of the route?" Ruth asked.

"After Baton Rouge, the next major town is Biloxi, Mississippi," I said. "We skirt Mobile, Alabama, head north on 65 to Montgomery, then Columbus, Georgia, Macon, and Wrightsville."

We agreed to confer with the Don on a base for the second and third nights. Ideally, we'd stop within easy driving distance of our final destination but not raise any alarms with the Judge and his people.

From there, the rest of that day involved equal parts packing and napping. I placed a rush order with Luther for Holy Water hollow points while Ruth and Olivia shopped for food and drink necessities.

Before sunrise the next morning one of Eugenio's drivers arrived to pick up Dex and Johnny. The men planned to spend the day at the hacienda working on the coach before driving it to our place after sunset.

The first errand on my list involved dragging Olivia to the phone store to get her on the company plan. She had an iPhone, but no service. Olivia protested until I explained that having her out of the communication loop on the road wasn't in anyone's best interest.

The guy at the store regarded her iPhone 3 with disdainful eyes. "You have a couple of upgrades on your account," he told me. "We can *totally* get your friend into a 6 or 6 Plus."

"Sure," I said, "which one do you want, Olivia?"

To my surprise, the woman's eyes lit up. "The 6 Plus, please," she said, adding sheepishly. "It has a better camera."

We'd walked to the store, which was about six blocks from my building. On the way home, Olivia snapped a series of pictures that beautifully captured the funky, rundown industrial quality of our neighborhood.

"You're good," I said, thumbing through the images. "You even managed to make a fire hydrant look interesting. Why did you take a picture of this grinning guy in the alley? And why the hell is he wearing a jacket in Texas in the summer?"

Olivia took the phone back. I couldn't see her eyes behind the enormous sunglasses, but her face paled. "I didn't see him when I took the picture," she said in a tight voice. "He completely ruined the shot."

The reaction seemed over the top for a photo bomber in a practice shot, but since I don't have an artistic sensibility in my body, I let it go. "What were you aiming at?" I asked instead.

"The slanting shadow of the building," she said in a more normal voice. "I like to play with lines and light. I used to have a sweet Nikon DSLR, but I had to sell it for rent money."

When somebody confesses they've fallen on hard times, sympathy doesn't do them a damned bit of good. "You really sucked it up and handled all the crap flying at you," I said. "Good for you."

"It was either that or lay down and be a victim," Olivia replied, determination filling the words. "I *refuse* to be a victim."

Good to know. When things went south in Georgia — which they surely would — she was going to need that attitude.

20

Dex sent me a text message when he and Johnny were a few blocks from the office. We all filed out to the alley, hearing the roar of the coach's motor before we saw the cool bluish LED headlights.

The guard light by the dumpster reflected off the machine's polished ebony exterior. I took one look at the RV and promptly christened it "The Hearse." Johnny was not amused.

When the door wooshed open, three steps automatically descended. We climbed single file into "the lounge," an area that reminded me of a Vegas high roller suite. Beyond that lay what I made the mistake of calling a "galley kitchen."

With a smug smile on his pale, patrician face, Johnny flipped a switch. The kitchen started to move.

"In the design parlance of the industry this area is referred to as a 'slide,'" he said. "The total coach contains three such extensions."

I looked at Ruth. "Did he really say, 'design parlance?'"

"He did," she said, shaking her head. "Boys with their toys."

That statement elicited a flood of vampiric outrage. Johnny spent the next 15 minutes lecturing us about the mechanical and technological marvels of The Hearse, emphasizing sharply that a machine of this caliber could not and *should not* be referred to as a 'toy.'

Looking over at Dex sprawled in one of the tufted leather captain's chairs in the cockpit, I asked, "How does it drive?"

"Like an aircraft carrier," he replied complacently, "but there's some heart under the hood. She'll hold her own with the 18-wheelers."

Music to my ears. I dreaded the thought of chugging to Georgia at 50 mph.

Under Ruth's direction, Olivia and I stocked the rest of The Hearse, familiarizing ourselves with the machine's nooks and crannies in the process.

Dex and I would sleep in the master bedroom to the rear, while Ruth claimed the second bedroom situated in one of the slides. Johnny planned to camp out full time in the lounge with his beloved computers.

Olivia took the cubicle across from Ruth, which was outfitted with a roomy bunk bed, built-in dresser, tiny closet, and a personal TV. The cozy nook seemed to please her, but the arrangement looked too claustrophobic for my tastes.

Since Helen and Ernest didn't need physical accommodations, Johnny had been right: we had more room than we could possibly use, but we would certainly be comfortable.

The next morning as the rising sun turned the night sky to robin's egg blue, I locked the building's back door and triggered the alarm system.

Normally I would have used my Dad's old line. "Anybody need to go before we hit the road?" but The Hearse had a bigger bathroom than the one in my apartment.

Johnny and Dex flipped for who would drive first. The vampire lost, settling down in the co-pilot's chair with thinly disguised disappointment.

Dex lowered the driver's window and looked down at me. "Straight out of town on 10 to Houston, right?"

"Right," I said. "You want me to take the lead or push the drag?"

"Push the drag," he said. "If we let you get out front, we won't see you again until we stop in Louisiana."

Planting my hands on my hips, I said, "Are you insinuating I drive too fast?"

"I'm not insinuating a damn thing," he said, hitting the ignition and bringing the coach's engines to life, "I'm coming right out and saying it."

My incredibly adult response? I stuck my tongue out at him before I walked to the Jeep and climbed behind the wheel. From the passenger seat, Ruth said, "Did he tell you not to drive too fast?"

"He did," I said. "We have been instructed to follow."

"Why do I have a feeling that arrangement may change when we hit the interstate?" she asked knowingly.

"Because you're clairvoyant?"

With a full-throated laugh, she said, "I don't need to be a psychic to know how well you respond to being told to fall in line."

Ernest opted to ride in The Hearse, which he had inspected at a minute level, flowing into the vents and creeping through the cracks and crevices as only a column of smoke can.

We weren't sure exactly where he'd be hanging out for the trip, but he promised not to do anything that would give surrounding motorists the idea that RV had caught fire.

Ruth and I invited Olivia to ride with us, but she preferred to stay in the coach, adding almost apologetically, "I'll join you later in the day."

When she said that, Helen announced her intent to watch TV in the lounge as the miles rolled away. My ghostly bestie wasn't fooling me. She was staying in The Hearse to keep an eye on Olivia.

We barely cleared the edge of the city, however, before Helen blipped into the Jeep's backseat.

"What you chicas doing back here?" she chirped brightly.

Ruth startled, hitting her head on the roof. I briefly swerved into the next lane, eliciting a middle finger and a burst of silent profanity from an adjacent car. The guy got the same gesture in return and a not so silent response.

"*Selby!*" Helen scolded. "Language!"

"*Helen!*" I responded, glaring at her in the rear-view mirror, "Warning!"

She did, at least, have the good grace to look ashamed. "Sorry," she said, "but the guys are boring me to tears up there. How can someone born in the 18th century be that interested in a freaking engine?"

Rubbing the top of her head, Ruth said, "*That* someone can be interested in anything mechanical. Especially if he can link that something to a computer."

"You can say that again," Helen whined. "When I finally decided to bail, he was compiling a spreadsheet on his iPad to analyze historical data on fuel consumption."

I rolled my eyes. "Only Johnny could turn 'miles per gallon' into historical fuel consumption data.' What's Olivia doing?"

"Sleeping," Helen said. "I guess all the late hours over the last couple of days wore her out."

Ruth twisted in her seat. "Do you think anything's wrong with her?"

"No," Helen said. "She told me her energy isn't good in the mornings. Later in the day she starts feeling stronger."

Later in the day. As in closer to sunset. Yet another vampiric trait surfacing.

Shortly before noon, we stopped in the parking lot of a

deserted filling station to have lunch. I noticed Ruth talking quietly to Olivia.

The other woman looked sleepy but seemed to perk up after two roast beef sandwiches — heavy on the beef, light on the lettuce and tomato.

Back on the road, and once again alone with Ruth, I asked, "How's Olivia?"

"We have to stay on her about the meat consumption," Ruth replied, "especially when she's tired. She needs the protein."

I made a mental note to make sure Dex grilled steaks for supper, but before I could give voice to the thought, Ruth struck.

"So," she said. "We're alone. Helen won't be popping in for the rest of the afternoon because I heard you ask her to stay close to Olivia. You owe me a story."

You know what they say: you can run, but you can't hide.

In the end, driving made the conversation I'd been avoiding much easier to navigate. I kept my eyes focused straight ahead, avoiding the painful intimacy of direct eye contact. Even my trust in Ruth couldn't offer enough anesthetic for the tale I had to share.

I GREW up 110 miles southwest of San Antonio in the Spinach Capital of the World — Crystal City, Texas.

Go ahead. Laugh. We even have a statue of Popeye, the spinach-eating cartoon character, under a tin shed in the median between East and West Zavala Streets.

My activist, hippie parents, Liz and Frank Manners moved there in 1976 to work with the Chicano civil rights movement for organized labor reform. In particular, they supported the La Raza Unida party, which was considered a dangerous, radical group of "foreigners" by the conservative locals.

My older brother, Dylan, and I took a lot of crap at school, but thanks to Liz and Frank's politics and the company they kept, I also got Helena de la Garza for a best friend. In the warmth of her tight-knit family I found a welcome refuge from the relentless political climate at our house.

Yeah, I have a brother. He'd already hit the road when all the bad shit went down. He's still out there somewhere living the free-spirited life of a vagabond. I haven't talked to him since Dad's funeral.

To understand the fateful choice my mother made that led to my "condition," you need at least a vague understanding of the complicated strains of prejudice, racial loyalty, and social discord in the desolate community of 8,000 plus.

Helen and I went to school on a campus that occupied the site of a massive World War II internment camp that, between 1943 and 1946, housed thousands of German, Italian, and Japanese detainees.

That community experience, coupled with a generational antipathy toward Mexican-Americans, caused a lot of people in town to nurse grudges against folks they saw as the ominous "other."

As the mile markers between San Antonio and Houston fell behind us that day, Ruth made it easy for me to keep talking. She only interrupted with pertinent, but infrequent questions while offering a quiet, supportive presence.

Without that, I'm not sure I would have been willing to allow my thoughts to return to my childhood home — a rented, slightly run-down ranch-style house not far from the Sacred Heart Church.

Rather than drag out the narrative, I said, "My mother made a deal with a *bruja negra.* By that time my parents had been living in Crystal City for 16 years. She was out of patience with the racial injustices and tensions. She wanted the power to compel change."

"What were the terms of the contract?" Ruth asked.

Swallowing hard, I said, "My mother made a highly specific pact to gain supernatural powers. Crystal City is in Zavala County."

Ruth's sharp intake of breath told me she knew what I was talking about. "La Lechuza?"

The Owl Witch.

Keeping my eyes trained forward, I nodded.

"That's the magic infecting your system?"

"Yes."

"Have you ever shifted?"

Blinking back tears, I said, "No. Helen's grandmother, Maria, helped me to prevent that."

I didn't have to add, *"But it's always possible."* Ruth knew that part already.

"Tell me how it happened," she said. "I have to know if I'm going to help you."

21

A shift foreman at the cannery died first — one with a reputation for sexually harassing women. The night watchman found the body in the company parking lot ripped open from throat to belt buckle.

The local grapevine went wild with speculation about the murder weapon, which appeared to have three blades. The equidistant incisions at the base of the man's neck grew closer as they traveled across the chest and into the soft belly tissue.

At the point of exit, the killer left a gaping hole through which the victim's viscera splayed out over the asphalt.

That afternoon when Helen and I showed up at her grandmother's house for after-school tortillas, we found her *abuela*, Maria, sitting at the kitchen table with a circle of old women.

As the screen door banged behind us, I heard the phrase "*La Lechuza*" for the first time as all the women superstitiously crossed themselves.

The scene around the table that day wasn't unusual. We were used to finding Maria and her friends drinking beer in the late afternoon and smoking acrid, unfiltered cigarettes. Those old ladies were badasses in house dresses; we adored them.

Maria was our rock — a haven of complete love, security, and acceptance amid the turbulence of teenage angst. She cooked for us, guarded us like an aged lioness, and taught us the legends and superstitions of her Spanish heritage.

In fractured English, Maria issued dire warnings about the unseen perils lurking in the world. She spoke scornfully of young people who gave up the old ways in the name of modernity all the while exposing themselves to evil influences.

With complete seriousness Maria instructed us about the ever-present danger of the *mal de ojo* or evil eye. She showed us the full glass of water atop her ancient Frigidaire that kept malevolent spirits at bay.

No one in her family would have dared incur bad luck by putting a hat on a bed nor would they point at a rainbow for fear of pimples erupting on the tips of their noses. She swore that eating chocolate took away the pain of being stung by a scorpion. I had a better solution; avoid scorpions in the first place.

Helen and I never tested any of Maria's theories. We went along with her lessons rather than endure blistering lectures in rapid-fire Spanish. I didn't believe a word of any of that "nonsense." At least not until the mention of *La Lechuza* turned my blood to ice.

I don't know how I knew in that moment that my mother was the Owl Witch, I just *knew*.

Dropping my books on the kitchen counter, I excused myself and went to the bathroom to throw up.

No one, not even Helen, knew I overheard my parents arguing about my mother cutting a deal with a *bruja.*

As I sat on the edge of the tub in the tiny pink bathroom, a knock sounded at the door. "*Qué está mal*, Selby?" Maria called out softly.

When I started to cry, she let herself in, perching beside me as I blurted out the whole story.

Looking back now, I shouldn't have been surprised by my mother's actions. My parents had always been passionate people, but of the two, Mom was the firebrand.

She walked the picket lines at the cannery, agitated at the school board meetings, and worked tirelessly as a political organizer.

Dad nursed a quieter commitment to social justice — driving people to the polls, providing translation services, or helping with the heavy hand of *La Migra*, the immigration officers.

But that afternoon in Maria's bathroom I couldn't have summoned up an analytical thought to save my life. I was scared out of my goddamn mind.

"Do you think my Mom killed that man?" I choked out, as Maria put her arm around me and drew my head down to her shoulder.

"I do not know, *hija*," she said, "but tonight you and Helena sleep here."

That one night turned into two weeks as the discovery of one mangled corpse after another sent the town into a terrified panic. Rumors swirled about a deranged serial killer on the loose or some rabid marauding animal prowling the streets.

After the fifth murder, Dad showed up at Maria's. He looked like he hadn't slept in days. He brought a suitcase filled with my clothes and personal things.

"Stay with Maria," he ordered me. "You'll be safe here while your mother and I work out some things at home."

"What things?" I asked stubbornly.

The black circles under his eyes made him look both tired and old. "Things I can't explain to you. Don't come back to the house until I tell you it's safe."

He shouldn't have said that.

The quickest way to get a teenager to do something is to *forbid* them to do it.

It took me a few nights to work up the courage, but ultimately, I snuck out of Maria's and went home.

When I got to that part in my narrative to Ruth, I had to stop and swallow hard several times. My friend waited patiently until I regained most of my composure.

"I went through the alleys so no one would see me," I said at last, gripping the steering wheel with white knuckles. "When I came into the backyard, I found my parents standing on the patio. Mom had started to shift. Her arms had already turned into giant wings. She must have heard me, because she rotated her head all the way around on her neck and looked at me with glowing violet eyes."

My stomach lurched at the memory. I saw it all again: my mother's head twisted at an unnatural angle, her shoulders quaking under the force of the transformation, the erupting feathers that shredded her clothes to rags as she grew into an enormous owl.

"She knew me," I said, "but she couldn't or wouldn't stop the transformation. When she screamed and turned on me, Daddy . . . he . . . he got in the way."

Hot tears rolled down my cheeks. Sometimes I still hear that scream in my nightmares. Ruth reached across the space between us and touched my arm. "You don't have to tell me this part."

I shook my head. "No. I'm only going to talk about this one time. Daddy tackled her, and she turned on him, tearing him apart with her talons. I remember the first cut on his cheek. He was wearing a white shirt, but it wasn't white anymore. My mother . . . that thing . . . had him on the ground finishing the job. I would have been next if Don Eugenio hadn't showed up."

"Don Eugenio was there?" Ruth asked with surprise.

"The killings in Crystal City caused problems throughout his territory," I said. "The vampires don't like it when the humans start asking the wrong questions. Eugenio went to the town to find La Lechuza and kill her. Instead, he tackled Mom and threw her back against the wall of the house to save me. Rather than face a pissed off vampire, she flew away into the night. I've never seen her again. Eugenio picked me up and carried me to Maria's. Turns out Helen's grandmother had more connections than we realized. When Maria checked me for injuries, she discovered scratches on my shoulder."

My parents were the last official victims of the Crystal City Killer. Since Mom was never found, the authorities assumed she'd been kidnapped and murdered. We buried Dad a week later under a double stone bearing both of their names.

At the service, I stood between Maria and Helen, my body racked with fever and chills. The other mourners assumed I was in shock. They weren't wrong.

No one questioned my absence at school for the remainder of the term. No one knew the hours Maria spent teaching me to control the poison in my system, to stop the violet fire before it reached my eyes, and to calm the contractions that threatened to turn me into a monster.

She also helped me to understand the altered course of my life.

"You will never be who you were before La Lechuza marked your body," Maria told me. "*El Señor* has given you a new reason to live. You must learn to help others as I have helped you."

With the weight of my story hanging thick in the air, Ruth said, "That's how you began to work with the paranormal?"

"Yes," I said. "I lived and studied with Maria until I graduated from high school. Then she sent me to San Antonio to learn from a more advanced teacher. Helen and I were on our way to Crystal City for the weekend when we had the car accident and she was killed. After that, I went into private investigations. You can find out a hell of a lot for a client when you have a ghost working the surveillance. Then I met Johnny and we went into business together. Dex and I married about a year after that. Four years later, the werewolf killed him."

"You've had a hard life," Ruth said quietly.

"Everybody has a hard life," I replied, my voice strained and thick. "Not once during any of that did my eyes turn violet. Why is this shit back now? Was it being in the presence of the Virgin Mary or did that asshole Shadow Man do this to me?"

"I don't know," Ruth admitted, "but we will find out. Together."

"Thank you," I said, my voice breaking. "Maria and Carmen, the woman I studied with in San Antonio, are both dead now."

"You're not alone, Selby," Ruth assured me. "We will get to the bottom of this. Do you still feel you can control the effects of the magic?"

"For now," I said, "but we don't exactly know what we're about to get ourselves into. You have to promise me something, Ruth."

"What?"

"No matter what you have to do, don't let me hurt anyone I love."

"Selby . . ."

"Promise me," I said urgently. "I've seen what La Lechuza can do. If I ever turn into that thing, kill me."

22

Once Ruth gave me her word, we made a point of changing the subject. Ruth knows me well enough to understand I needed to get a handle on my emotions before seeing the others. By the time we stopped for the night, I'd managed to lock the old memories back in their cages where they belong. I was tired, but I had it together.

Right at sunset we followed the Hearse as it turned off the interstate and headed down a country road. Fifteen minutes later, Johnny maneuvered the massive vehicle along a two-rut dirt lane with barely enough room between the fence posts to allow the coach to pass.

At the end of the lane, he pulled to a stop next to a dilapidated barn. I cut the Jeep's engine a few yards off to the right. Ruth and I both leaned forward and looked out the windshield.

"Home sweet home," she said.

"It's not bad," I said. "I expected to be camping on the bank of some bayou swamp with gators inviting themselves to supper."

Ruth's eyes swept over the dense tree growth, drinking in the familiar landscape. "I made sure we'd be too far away from water to worry about gators," she said, "but there are plenty of other things living in there."

As I opened my door and stepped out, I unconsciously felt for the Glock in its shoulder holster under my jacket. "They don't bother us," I said, "and we won't bother them."

Silently I hoped "them" could be stopped by bullets if "they" were in a mood to be bothersome.

To my surprise, Johnny was already plugging a power cable from The Hearse into a covered electrical outlet mounted to a pole outside the barn.

"What is this place?" I asked Ruth.

"The land belongs to my cousin, Louis," she explained. "He used to rebuild cars out here. That's why there's power and water. It's so remote we shouldn't have to worry about visitors."

Swatting at a mosquito busily drawing a pint of plasma off my forearm, I said, "Maybe not human visitors, but there are more than enough of these damn things."

With a wicked grin, Ruth said, "Let me fix that."

She stepped away from me and closed her eyes. Within seconds, I felt a current of power emanate from the witch.

Johnny stopped what he was doing and grew utterly still, his eyes fixed on Ruth. A faint light rose from her body and her lips moved with the words of an incantation none of us could hear.

I don't know what I expected would happen, maybe a series of flashes from a mojo-infused bug zapper. Instead, a wave of something passed through me. A pale dome of energy settled over The Hearse and the surrounding clearing.

Beyond the translucent barrier, confused clouds of mosquitoes buzzed angrily. Ruth raised her hand, waving elegant fingers toward the insects in a hushing motion. The miniscule bloodsuckers fell silent as Ruth opened her eyes, which pulsated slightly in the gathering darkness.

"What the hell did you just do?" I asked.

She smiled, her accent heavy on her tongue. "*Lutte contre les ravageurs, ma chérie.*"

Pest control? All I could think was, *"There are some cockroaches back home living on borrowed time."*

Dex and Johnny pulled out camp chairs from a bin under the bus, which also sheltered an extendable grill. Olivia stood at the edge of the energy barrier studying the scene in the gathering twilight.

Helen floated up beside her and said, "This must be pretty different from New England."

Olivia nodded, "Everything down here seems so wild and alive."

As if to prove her point, a phalanx of mosquitoes made a dive at the faintly glowing dome. All they succeeded in doing was splattering themselves against its surface.

"Eww," Helen said. "Gross or what?"

Thankfully the tiny corpses winked out of sight or we'd have been dining under one giant dirty windshield.

While the boys prepared vegetable skewers and steaks, I built a campfire — a real one, not some flick-of-the-switch fire pit imitation. Ernest hovered behind me offering far more advice than I needed.

When the wood caught, the wildfire elemental slid into the flames, reveling in his native environment. Aware that he had an audience, Ernest started literally playing with fire.

Flickering orange and yellow castles rose on the stacked logs as troops marched upward from the coals toward the fortresses. As the mock battle commenced, archers unleashed fiery arrows that sent sparks shooting toward the stars.

Ernest put on such an entrancing show that when the largest castle fell, and the victorious troops set up a cheer, we joined our voices with theirs in appreciation of the elemental's entertainment skills. He emerged from the wisps of smoke with a shy smile on his shadowy "face."

"Did you enjoy it?" he asked.

"Ernest," Ruth said admiringly, "you are an artist. That looked like a real battle from history."

Floating into one of the folding chairs, Ernest assumed the shape of a relaxed camper. "It *was* a real battle," he said. "I don't remember the name of the town, but it happened in the Middle Ages."

"How long have you been around?" I asked him.

Ernest's form undulated. "A really long time," he said finally.

That vague answer wasn't going to cut it in the campfire confessional. "What's your first memory?"

With none of the usual glib bravado in his voice, Ernest said, "My kind was born from the explosion of a great volcano when the planet was young. The force of life roamed the earth freely in those days."

Before I could say anything else, Olivia asked, "When you say the 'force of life,' do you mean God?"

"Beats me," the elemental shrugged. "One day the light of consciousness filled us and many other creatures as well, almost as if the life force was trying out forms and shapes to see what would work best."

Damn. Ernest dated back to the evolutionary drawing board. The way he described it, elementals were a design that didn't make the cut. The prototypes, however, kept right on ticking through the millennia.

Fortunately Dex took that moment to announce the steaks were ready because Ernest had left me with a lot to think about and little to say. In those few minutes, the elemental moved up several notches in my estimation — from wisecracking sidekick to a being who witnessed the formation of the earth.

Maybe sharing my story with Ruth triggered my reaction,

but sometimes, even with all the complications, I'm hit with what an awesome life I've been given. I gained my paranormal awareness at tremendous personal cost, but that doesn't diminish the wonder of experiencing what most humans refuse to believe exists.

After we ate, Helen announced her plan to "pay some calls."

"On who?" I asked, arching my eyebrows with surprise.

"There's a cemetery across the main road outside the gate," she said. "It would be rude for me to be so close and not say hello."

Before I could ask anything else, she blipped out of sight.

Ghost etiquette. Who knew?

Dex passed out more cold beer and we settled around the fire to let our food digest.

"This is nice," Olivia said. "If we weren't on our way to find my evil vampiric great-grandfather, we could be . . ."

She caught herself and looked down shyly.

"Friends," Ruth finished for her. "A group of friends on a camping trip."

Olivia nodded. "I realize we haven't known each other for long and this started as a business relationship, but I've come to like you all so much. It's been a long time since I had any friends."

"Why?" Ruth asked, adding, "If that's not too personal of me to ask."

"It's not," Olivia said. "When you have the kind of illness people can't see, everyone starts thinking you're crazy. Not at first, but before long it happens. When you've cancelled on them for the second or third time, or tried to explain that yes, a walk in the gardens would be beautiful, but your eyes can't take that much light. Before you know it, you're staying in your pajamas for days and sleeping way too much."

"That's called depression," Ruth said gently.

Taking a pull on her Dos Equis, Olivia said, "It is. But at some point, at least for me, anger and impatience took over. I wanted answers. So here I am with my new friends dealing with those answers. Be careful what you ask for, little girl."

She smiled when she cracked the joke, waving the top of her bottle toward each of us in a mock toast we all returned on a wave of rueful laughter.

Rather than run the risk of things getting too serious, I said with exaggerated gravity, "Yes, here we are. Under our big ole supernatural bug shield."

That touched off the kind of laughs that had everyone wiping their eyes.

When I finally caught my breath, I said, "Honestly. I don't think I've ever enjoyed being outside this much. Come on, Ruth, out with it. You're not just holding back the flying pests, are you? All the bugs are gone."

Still chuckling, Ruth ran a fine-boned hand through her thick hair. "Guilty," she said. "I grew up closer to New Orleans. If you think the bugs are bad here, you don't want to know what comes crawling out of those bayous. The spell I used tonight was one of the first my grandmother taught me to cast."

"Your grandmother was like you?" Olivia asked.

A look filled with love and longing came into Ruth's eyes. "Granny wasn't like me. Or maybe I should say I'm not like her. No matter how much I wish I were."

Touching the back of her hand for only a fraction of a second, Johnny said. "Tell us about your *grand-mère, s'il vous plaît*."

Ruth's voice rose and fell in rhythm to the crackling fire. She told us about her grandmother, Genevieve Beauchene — and then she talked about her father, Rene.

I still shiver when I think about the story she told us that night, in part because I know she told it to make me feel better.

"You will burn, girl," Rene screamed at his daughter. "You killed your Mama and you will burn in hell for your sins."

Ruth turned her face into her grandmother's shoulder to shut out the sight of her father's contorted features gone purple with rage. She felt Genevieve's arms tighten protectively around her, a small current of power passing from the older woman's body into Ruth's, calming and warming her.

"Leave my house, Rene," Genevieve said, her voice rough with threat. "Do not make me forget that you are my son."

"Or what, Mama?" Rene snarled, the smell of whiskey souring his breath. "You'll throw the chicken bones and curse me? How in the name of the sweet Lord and Savior can I be more cursed than I already am? My Colette is dead, killed by that black-hearted devil you call my daughter. She is the child of Satan as I live and breathe."

"Go, Rene," Genevieve said. "I will not tell you again."

Muttering under his breath, the man half fell down the steps and staggered into the yard. Ruth heard the door of his pickup slam and the gravel in the driveway spin as he gunned the engine and fishtailed into the lane.

The sobs Ruth had held back broke in her chest. Her shoulders heaved from the force of the tears.

Genevieve spoke soothing words, humming low in her throat and rocking her granddaughter in her arms. A blanket of calm flowed over the child until she sighed and murmured, half awake, "I know what you're doing, Granny."

"All I'm doing is loving you, chéri,*" Genevieve whispered. "The magic only helps the love find the hurt places."*

When Ruth stopped talking, Johnny said, in a voice hoarse

with emotion, "You are most certainly like your dear *grand-mère*. Most certainly."

For several minutes we all stared into the fire and enjoyed the blackness of the night around us. We don't get those glittering splashes of stars in the city.

"Why did your father think you were the child of Satan?" Olivia asked suddenly.

"Because my family came under attack from an evil creature," Ruth explained. "My father didn't believe that I was his child, an idea made worse when my mother died giving birth to me. Rene Beauchene had no magic in his soul much less love in his heart. Grief, twisted religious beliefs, and cheap whiskey drove him out of his mind."

Olivia considered the words. "He knew you were different, like his mother, and it scared him."

"That's perceptive of you," Ruth said.

"I'd like to take credit," Olivia admitted, "but I only heard an echo of what you were thinking."

Normally, Ruth would never drop her mental shields like that, which told me how much sharing her story cost my friend. Our eyes met across the fire and I gave the witch an almost imperceptible nod of thanks, which she returned with equal subtlety.

"You are gaining control of your gifts," Johnny told Olivia approvingly.

With a hint of excitement in her voice, she asked, "What else do you think I can do?"

Johnny likes showing off creepy vampire shit almost as much as he likes playing with computers.

"Let us find out," he replied, shifting his attention to the inky blackness beyond the campfire. "There are forest creatures watching us. Can you identify them for me?"

Following his line of sight, I estimated that functional visibility dropped to zero less than ten yards out. Compared to what Olivia was about to do, I might as well have been legally blind.

Studying the patch of open ground I knew lay between us and the tree, her brow wrinkled in concentration. Finally, she said, "There's a raccoon at the edge of the woods."

That had to be a good 50 yards away. Not bad.

"What else?" Johnny asked.

"It's hard to see through the trees," Olivia said slowly, "but there are deer out there, too."

"Keep going," the vampire directed.

Olivia's eyes probed the distant shadows. "The land slopes down to a creek," she said, the words sounding far off and removed. "There's a skunk drinking at the water, and on the other side I see something that looks like a big rat with teeth."

"An opossum," Ruth murmured, fascinated.

"The land climbs again after that and on the crest of the hill there's a . . . a mountain lion," Olivia finished. "That's all I can see."

At the words "mountain lion," my hand reached for my pistol. Johnny's words stopped me. "Do not concern yourself, Selby," he said. "The cat in question walks away from us at a distance of five miles."

Olivia's head snapped around. I saw something in her eyes like the energy that had animated Ruth's gaze when she worked the barrier spell.

"Five *miles*?" Olivia said. "My eyes can see five miles into pitch darkness?"

I couldn't tell if the illumination washing over Johnny came from the fire or from some otherworldly flame burning deep within his soul.

Yeah, I know. Vampires aren't supposed to have souls, but

Johnny has one. It may be trapped by his existence, but I'm convinced it's in there.

"With your eyes, *madame*, and with your mind," he whispered, speaking from that deep place where he contains his true essence. "The night holds no dominion over us."

Damn. What was I saying about creepy vampire shit?

23

Helen's form slowly appeared outside the rusted wrought iron fence surrounding the country graveyard. At one time a matching pair of gates must have guarded the dead. Nothing remained of that elegant touch, however, except a pair of broken hinges dangling from each of the tall posts holding up a curved sign.

Levitating herself so she could read the letters head on, Helen's faint glow illuminated the words, "Cyprus Cemetery."

Below her on the dirt road a Creole woman's voice called up to her, "Child, what you doing up there?"

Descending smoothly, Helen found herself in the company of a dark-skinned woman in a gingham dress. A dusty length of maroon cloth encircled her head, knotted on one side with the ends left long to lay flat against the material.

"What's that on your head?" Helen asked.

The woman laughed, running a translucent hand along the edge of the cloth. "Where you from that you never seen a tignon?"

"Texas," Helen answered.

The Creole's eyes narrowed. "Texas when?"

"Since I've been dead, I don't really keep track, but I think it's 2015. Why?"

"'Cause I been laying in this earth since 1852, that's why," the woman said. "Power down there cross the road done woke me up tonight, me and all the others."

Helen looked into the cemetery and saw spirits milling among the stones. Long flat slabs of granite covered many of the graves as if to hold the deceased down.

Balls of light danced around the older, taller headstones, sometimes shooting up into the overhanging tree branches.

Following Helen's gaze, the Creole said, "They think they gonna shoot up to heaven doing that, but it don't work that way."

Remembering her manners, Helen extended her hand. "My name's Helen," she said. "I'm traveling with my friends camped down the lane by that old barn. What's your name?"

"Mathilde," the woman said. "Who them people you with?"

"My friends," Helen repeated.

The old ghost eyed her suspiciously. "You keep company with the living dead?" she asked. "There a vampire down that road."

Not sure how to answer, Helen finally said, "Yeah, but he's a *French* vampire. That's better, right?"

To her surprise, Mathilde laughed. "It make no difference if the teeth going in your neck be French or not. You gonna be dead all the same."

Helen shook her head vigorously. "Johnny would never kill anyone." Then, correcting herself, she said, "Well, he hasn't killed anyone since 1919, but that was a war thing. The French and the Germans weren't getting along. At all."

Mathilde nodded. "I know about that war. Men buried in there went off to fight in it. How come a being from another place going around with a vampire and a witch?"

"A being from another place?" Helen said. "Oh, you must

mean Dex. He's my best friend's husband. He hasn't been back from . . . wherever . . . for very long. The vampire, Johnny, is Selby's business partner."

"This Selby, she the witch?"

"No, that would be Ruth. She's from Louisiana. Down around New Orleans, I think."

Closing her eyes, Mathilde seemed to be directing her concentration toward the campsite. "She got the conjure of Marie Laveau in her veins," the woman said at last.

"Marie Laveau was a voodoo woman, right?"

Mathilde grinned, "Was? Don't you be thinking Marie gone for good. There three women down there. Who the third one?"

"Oh, that's Olivia. She hired Selby and the others to help her figure out what's wrong with her."

"Ain't no mystery about what wrong with that girl," Mathilde said grimly. "She done got herself caught halfway between heaven and hell. Be better for her if she don't never go nowhere near Georgia."

"Why?" Helen asked.

"Cause the devil himself sitting there waiting for her.

BEFORE WE WENT to bed everyone agreed we didn't have to hit the road at the crack of dawn — everyone except Johnny. He voted for a 5 a.m. departure. The rest of us who actually *sleep* soundly voted him down.

I woke up at dawn anyway.

As I lay in the dark listening to Dex snoring softly beside me, I had the strong conviction I'd been the victim of some kind of vampire-based alarm clock, but I couldn't prove it.

I gave up after about 20 minutes. Slipping out of bed, I

dressed and exited into the lounge, pulling the bedroom door closed behind me.

Johnny had arranged three huge laptops with illuminated keyboards on the table. He stared at the screens absorbed in his work and what was likely Beethoven being piped straight into his brain via a pair of Bose headphones.

He didn't look away, but his hand automatically offered me a massive thermal coffee mug. Three others sat on the counter beside him waiting for their intended owners to wake up.

Johnny may have groused about "wasting valuable driving time on sleep," but he'd brewed java for the mortals anyway.

The vampire's skills with a coffee grinder cancel out the annoyance of his occasional bitchy moods. For a dedicated tea drinker, Johnny makes a cup of Joe that would reduce a Starbucks barista to tears of envious admiration.

Leaving him to his laptops, I opened the coach door. The sun wasn't really up, but a delicate layer of pink rimmed the horizon. Cool air greeted me along with a chorus of bird songs from the woods.

In the weak light, I made out Ruth's energy shield still at work keeping the creepy crawlies on their side of the magical line. Secure in the knowledge I wouldn't get eaten alive by chiggers or ticks, I went through a series of stretches before beginning my tai chi routine.

I took up the discipline after Dex died in an effort to calm my mind with something that didn't involve tequila. At first, I wasn't sure the choreographed movements did anything other than shorten my hangovers, but then I came to rely on those few calm minutes each morning.

Some people can sit still for hours and meditate. I have to move. So far, I've only found three things that will put me in the magic "flow" state: target practice, cleaning my gun, and tai chi.

Yes, I am aware that one of these things is not like the others. Sue me. I excel at being a study in contrasts.

Several minutes later, when I finished the final sequence, I realized Helen was half sitting / half floating in one of the folding chairs watching me.

"There you are," I said. "Were you out all night?"

She made a face that looked vaguely like a cat about to toss a hairball. "Good with the mom impersonation there, Selb. And a cheerful good morning to you, too. Aren't you supposed to be all Zen and chill after tai chi?"

Moving to join her, I said, "I'm chill enough, thank you very much."

Helen rolled her eyes. "With a line like that I'm surprised you didn't come outside with curlers on your head."

Even in Texas, the land of perpetual big hair, I can assure you that not Helen or anyone else has ever seen me in curlers. Most days I run my fingers through my hair and call it done.

"You missed one hell of a show around the campfire last night," I said. "Johnny was in full vampire mojo mode and Olivia kept up pretty damn well."

I described the supernatural tutoring session we witnessed, but when I got to the part about the mountain lion Helen interrupted the story with an outraged squeal.

"You could have *warned* me!" she said. "What kind of friend leaves a friend in a cemetery to be *cat chow*?"

Sometimes when Helen's on a roll, she forgets her less than physical state.

"You're a ghost," I said levelly. "Mountain lions don't eat ectoplasm."

That stymied her for a nanosecond before she went on the offensive. "How do you know it wasn't some kind of big black ghost cat like they see over in England all the time?"

Since Helen has been on the other side she's made cryptozoology her hobby — or at least *talking* about cryptozoology. She's given voice to amorphous claims about being able to see Bigfoot and shit like that, but until Helen walks in the door with Chewbacca following her, I'm not buying it.

"Fine," I said, conceding the point more to get her to move along than in an expression of agreement. "I should have warned you. Who or what did you find in the graveyard?"

Helen's demeanor instantly grew somber. "There are some *really* old dead people over there, like back to Indians and French settlers and stuff. This one Creole lady met me at the gate and said *creepy* stuff."

"Like what?"

"She could sense everyone down here and wanted to know why we were all traveling together."

If the dead woman had heard Dex and Johnny arguing about one another's driving skills, she would have wondered even more.

"What was her name?"

"Mathilde," Helen said. "She told me she came to this country from Martinique before the Civil War. We talked almost all night. I think she may have been a voodoo queen."

From behind us, Ruth said, "Not voodoo. Most likely she was a practitioner of quimbois."

"Morning," I said, as she claimed one of the empty chairs. "What's quimbois?'

Ruth explained that the system of herbal medicine, spiritual healing, and sorcery known as quimbois existed alongside Catholicism on Martinique for hundreds of years.

"The tradition fostered many powerful practitioners," she said. "It sounds like you met one last night, Helen."

"I've never seen so much energy in such a small cemetery," Helen agreed. "I could see most of the ghosts, but then there were these balls of light zipping around all over the place like fireworks or something."

Helen had been a people watcher when she was alive and apparently nothing had changed after her death. "Do you do this back home?" I asked. "Go to cemeteries and watch ghosts?"

Helen shrugged. "I have spirit friends in San Antonio," she said, "but I don't hang out in the graveyard. But since we're on a trip, this is like sightseeing for me. It's fun to hear stories from new people."

I couldn't get past the "spirit friends" announcement. That stopped me in mid-coffee sip. "You have ghost friends?"

"Well, *duh*," Helen said, rolling her eyes. "I'm not some weirdo introvert like you. I know lots of people on the other side. You ought to see the crowd that shows up every year on the anniversary of the fall of the Alamo. Those guys are so *not* over it, and all that 'Remember the Alamo' stuff doesn't help. But Davy Crockett? He's a hoot! Do you know he didn't really wear a coonskin cap?"

Thank God Ruth's bug shield was holding. The way my mouth dropped open, I could have swallowed half the insect population of Louisiana.

"Why am I just hearing about all this now?" I managed to croak.

Helen tossed her hair. "Because I'm a woman of mystery," she said in a *femme fatale* voice, "and I don't divulge my secrets."

"You haven't been able to keep a secret from me since kindergarten," I said, regretting the words the instant they left my mouth when I saw shades of guilt cloud her eyes.

Helen did keep a secret from me. For five years. She never told me that Dex was watching over me even when I asked her repeatedly if she had seen him.

"Sorry, babe," I said. "Sometimes I'm a dumbass."

In spite of my assurances that I'd forgiven her, Helen still worried that she'd betrayed our friendship with her silence.

In moments like that, I wanted nothing more than to be able to give my best friend a hug, or even punch her on the shoulder and tell her to get over her drama queen self, but I could do neither. Fortunately, nobody bounces back like my girl.

"How do you know I haven't been hiding a fabulous double life from you for decades?" she asked.

Wincing at the word "decades," I said, "Bullshit. Try again."

"Most of the spirits I know don't have living friends," Helen admitted, "and they don't want to because it makes them miss being alive too much. It really is a club you have to die to get into, honey. Don't be in a rush to get your membership card."

No argument there.

"This Mathilde could sense our presence?" Ruth asked.

Helen nodded. "She said you have the conjure of Marie Laveau in your veins."

Ruth's face registered surprise. "Did she now?" she said thoughtfully, looking up the lane toward the cemetery. "That's interesting."

"Marie Laveau as in 'black cat tooth and a mojo bone?'" I asked.

The three of us looked at one another for a heartbeat and then sang in bad harmony, "*Another man done gone*," before dissolving in laughter.

(Don't judge if you're too young to understand. Look it up. Bobby Bare. Very country. Killer lyrics. Moving on.)

"That would be the one," Ruth said, wiping her eyes. "Marie was a powerful voodoo queen. We are no relation, but all who practice workings in the Big Easy have been touched by her conjure. Madame Mathilde was correct about that."

"I hope that's all she was correct about," Helen said.

"What's that supposed to mean?" I asked.

"She told me we shouldn't take Olivia to Georgia because the devil himself was waiting for her."

(Yeah, there's a song about that one, too, but I won't go there.)

Ruth set her cup down and stood. "I must speak with this Mathilde."

"Wrong," I said, standing up as well. "*We* must speak with her."

From the door of the coach, Olivia said, "Then I'm coming, too."

This morning was just getting better and better.

24

Since she showed up on our doorstep, Olivia had agreed with whatever we suggested. In what world could that last, right? Standing in the door of the bus, Olivia heard everything Helen said about Mathilde.

What she heard made her determined to meet the Creole ghost in person. When Ruth and I suggested it might be better if Olivia remain behind while we checked out the graveyard, the woman's temper flared for the first time and we got a glimpse of her stubborn side.

When her jaw set in a hard line I knew we were in trouble.

"No," she said, flatly. She stepped out of the coach and approached us with short, determined steps. "I'm the one who decides what's good for me. I have to learn to live with what I am. I can't do that on second-hand reports. I want to hear what this Mathilde has to say."

On reflex I opened my mouth to argue. Ruth laid a hand on my arm. "Don't bother," she counseled wisely. "You'd say the same thing in her place."

Frustrated annoyance must have shown in my eyes because Ruth grinned. She knew she had me.

"You know I'm right," she said. "Olivia has seen what lies under the ordinary world. We have a responsibility to teach her. The same way Helen's *abuela* taught you."

Maria's voice moved through my thoughts. *"Someone must do this work."*

Unscrewing the top of my coffee mug, I drained the last of the contents.

"Fine," I said. "Who am I to stand in the way of a lousy idea?"

When I reached behind me to check the automatic snugged at the small of my back, Helen saw an opening to get in a zinger over my earlier mountain lion logic.

"Bullets don't work against ectoplasm, Selb," she said in a saccharin tone.

Rewarding her with a rude gesture, I said, "But they do work against snakes."

A shudder rippled through Helen's filmy form. Dead or alive, the girl hates snakes. Point for me.

Dex stuck his head out the bedroom window. "Do you want us to start packing up or wait until you hear what Mathilde has to say?"

What was this? International Eavesdropping Day?

"Wait," I said. "Have some breakfast with Mr. Prissy Fangs and keep him from blowing an artery over the delay."

Johnny's voice floated out the open coach door. "I have long ago resigned myself to the torture of your spontaneity and loose relationship with time, dear Selby."

Grumbling under my breath, I fell in beside Ruth and Olivia with Helen floating along. No one spoke. We allowed ourselves to enjoy the beautiful morning. Birds sang in the trees and when we turned into the main lane, a fox ran across the road eliciting an admiring gasp from Olivia.

The walk churned up enough friendly endorphins in my

head that when we reached the graveyard entrance, my irritation had passed.

We found the area completely deserted except for a mockingbird perched about the "C" in Cyprus.

"Now what?" I asked Ruth.

Olivia, who had been studying the bird, answered. "He wants us to go inside," she said. "He says Mathilde will find us."

"The *bird* told you that?" Helen asked. "*Cool!*"

"Hold on," I said. "That bird hasn't made a sound. How did he tell you anything?"

Without warning, the mockingbird let out with a furious squawk and dive bombed me, delivering a vicious peck to the top of my head before flying back to the top of the sign.

"He doesn't like your attitude," Olivia explained unnecessarily.

Checking my head for blood, I said, "I got that.

Smothering a smile, Ruth gestured toward the cemetery. "Shall we?"

"Lead off," I said. "I'm climbing the fence."

"Why would you do that?" Olivia asked.

"Because I don't trust your pal up there not to take a crap on my head, that's why," I said, putting my boot on the lower rung of the wrought iron and hoisting myself up.

Overhead, the mockingbird serenaded us with an excellent imitation of an all too human laugh.

Landing on the other side with a thud, I brushed the rust off my hands and rejoined the others. Though small and remote, the cemetery seemed well maintained. Only one or two modern markers broke up the rows of weathered, lichen-coated tombstones.

"Why are the graves covered in granite slabs?" Olivia asked, pulling her phone out to take pictures.

"They're called ledger stones," Ruth explained. "Many are

engraved with details of the person's life, but others are left blank. Some people think the stones are there to weight the casket in place in this wet soil or against other forces that might cause the dead to rise."

Olivia who had just taken a photo of Ruth standing by an ornately carved, weeping angel froze. "Other forces?"

"You said you wanted to learn," Ruth replied. "We call the magic of death necromancy. My grandmother had the power to call the dead from their graves."

Equal parts horror and fascination warred on Olivia's face. "Why would anyone want to raise the dead?"

A breath of wind lifted the ends of Ruth's hair as she answered. She allowed her power to come into her eyes in a display more potent than the one we saw the day before. I guessed that the witch wasn't just giving Olivia a taste of mojo; she was broadcasting a hello to Mathilde as well.

"Shrouds have no pockets," Ruth said, her voice low and sultry with the current running through her body, "but the dead carry secrets into the ground. The keys to untangling an inheritance, the revelation of a betrayal, the knowledge to right an old wrong."

About the time Olivia snapped her picture, I casually sat down on a grave covered with a raised brick box that may, in the past, have been meant to hold flowers. Absorbed in watching Ruth talk about necromancy, I wasn't ready for the voice that spoke almost in my ear.

"Mind your manners, girl. Don't you be sitting on folks' graves."

In a blur of motion, I sprang up drawing my automatic and training it on the ghost of an old woman in a headwrap who stood in the shadow of an ancient oak.

She threw her head back and laughed. "How you gonna

make ole Mathilde more dead, Selby Jensen? Silver hold no power over me."

"Jesus, lady," I said, lowering my weapon. "Was that really necessary?"

Mathilde cackled again. "Maybe no, but laughter be good for the soul."

Staring at the spirit, Olivia asked Ruth, "How am I able to see her?"

"Because she wants you to," Ruth answered. Then, switching to French, she greeted Mathilde.

The old woman answered in the same language, and then, reverting to English, said, "You are the witch."

"Yes," Ruth said, "and you are a quimboiseur."

The specter smiled and shook her head. "On Martinique, yes, but here in this land I have sat at the knee of them that work vodun and hoodoo." Then, holding a hand out to Olivia, she said, "Come to me, child."

Olivia slid her phone into her pocket and moved in front of Mathilde. "You know what I am, don't you?" she asked the Creole ghost.

"I know you are God's child," Mathilde answered. "Anything you do be part of His plan. He in all you do, good and bad. But remember, little one, fear gonna keep you alive. Fear just another name for wisdom. Listen to fear when it whisper in the night."

Moving closer, Ruth said, "Helen said you know what waits for us in Georgia. Can you tell us more about that?"

The ghost's eyes crinkled in thought. Finally she said, "Walk with old Mathilde, Ruth Beauchene. Only you.

Ruth glanced at me. "Go ahead," I said. "We'll wait."

As the witch and the ghost disappeared deeper into the cemetery, Olivia said, "Do you think she's right? That even this is part of God's plan?"

Making sure Mathilde was out of sight, I sat back down on the grave and patted the stone. Olivia joined me while Helen crossed her legs yoga style and floated on a level with us.

"At that girl's school you read about, we saw the Virgin Mary," I said. "She gathered the soul of that murdered girl and the souls of all the nameless children who died in that building over the years to herself."

I told her the whole story about the Shadow Man and the babies who rested among the roses.

"That night," I said, "when the Blessed Mother took the children away, after her radiance faded — well there was Dex." My voice roughened at the memory, and Olivia laid a comforting hand on my knee to encourage me to go on.

Normally I might have brushed aside the gesture, but out of the corner of my eye, I saw Helen reach for me as well, and then draw her hand back. Even after fifteen years, she still forgets sometimes that she's no longer alive. I let Olivia offer me comfort because in part, Helen wanted to and couldn't.

"If he hadn't been real," I went on, "or if he hadn't been able to stay, I didn't want to live anymore. Dex heard my thoughts and told me we'd do it my way. That's when he touched me, and I knew that whatever he was, whoever he was, didn't matter because I had him back. I won't lie to you. There's never been much between me and God, but He or She, gave me back the only man I've ever loved. So yeah, I do think what's happening to you could be part of a bigger plan."

Olivia nodded, staring after Ruth and Mathilde. "But why now?" she asked. "Even after all those tests Johnny ran on me, we still don't know why my differences didn't appear in childhood."

"Try to be patient," I replied. "If an old dead voodoo lady 600 miles from Wrightsville can sense part of what's up with you, imagine what we'll find out when we actually get there."

"That," Olivia said, "is what I'm worried about."

MATHILDE LED Ruth to a deserted corner of the cemetery and pointed to a simple headstone mostly hidden in tangled brambles.

"My bones sleep in that dirt," the spirit said.

Ruth looked down at the forgotten grave. "Why don't you rest?"

The ghost smiled. "You know the dead walk side by side with the living. Some of us still got business on this earth. Don't be playing dumb with ole Mathilde."

Ruth returned the smile. "You and my grandmother would have been great friends."

"I know 'bout Genevieve Beauchene," Mathilde said, "and I know about you, too."

"Then why draw us into the cemetery this morning?" Ruth said. "Why not come down to our fire last night and talk to me?"

"'Cause I needed you here," the Creole said. "I want you to take dirt from my grave with you to Georgia."

Bending to lay her hand on the warm earth, Ruth closed her eyes. "I feel your power," she said. "How would you have me use this dirt?"

"When the time come," Mathilde said, "you will know."

25

"She gave you a handful of dirt and then *disappeared*?" I glanced at Ruth out of the corner of my eye as I asked the question and saw her mouth quirk into a smile.

Ruth finds my lack of patience with all things metaphysical amusing. Obviously, I'm a believer or I wouldn't be in this line of work. It just bugs the hell out of me that entities like Mathilde can't be more direct.

The Creole spook's evasiveness sent us back to camp with dammed little to report. A ghost told us we're headed for trouble in Georgia. Not exactly a news flash — and certainly nothing that would cause us to change our plans for the day.

Now, however, we were back on the interstate *and* back on the subject of the graveyard encounter.

"Don't underestimate graveyard dirt," Ruth cautioned me. "It can be used in potent ways. Didn't Maria teach you that?"

Keeping my eyes on the road, I said, "No, but Helen and I have been schooled in roughly 9 jillion uses for eggs and safety pins."

"Eleven jillion," Helen piped in from the backseat where she and Olivia were pouring over shopping sites on an iPad they had commandeered from Johnny.

Chuckling, Ruth said, “We may need eggs and safety pins before this trip is over.”

We had declared our second day of travel Girl’s Day in the Jeep. Grabbing ample drinks and snacks, we left Johnny, Dex, and Ernest to their own devices in the Hearse.

With the subject of graveyard dirt on the table, Helen showed her post-mortem groupie colors. "What does graveyard dirt look like? Can we see it?"

I laughed at the sight of her disappointed face in the rearview mirror when Ruth held up a plastic bag filled with ordinary crumbling earth.

Olivia adopted a more academic approach, asking Ruth to explain the soil sample’s functional potential. Like all witches, Ruth loves to talk shop when she has a willing (or in this case, captive) audience; she answered in detail.

Graveyard dirt, when referred to as “goofer dust,” may be used as an ingredient in various workings designed to harm or even kill your enemies.

All manner of factors affect the potency and usefulness of the dirt: method of collection, time of day, phase of the moon. But the biggie? Grave occupant. According to Ruth, we hit the motherlode on that last part.

Because Mathilde offered *consent* as well as dirt, she gave Ruth a metaphysical nuclear weapon.

“That stuff isn’t going to go off in your purse or anything is it?” I asked suspiciously.

“No,” Ruth said. “I’m the only one who can use it. Don’t worry, this is not my first rodeo with graveyard dirt.”

Her reassurances left me feeling reasonably positive about our takeaway from the early morning cemetery visit — that feeling didn’t last long.

Around 11 o'clock I checked in with Dex to negotiate our lunch stop. The blaring music inside The Hearse forced me to hold the phone six inches from my ear.

"Is that *Earth, Wind, and Fire*?" I yelled into the microphone.

Dex roared back, "Yes. Ernest's turn to pick the music. It's better than what Johnny had on."

"Let me guess. Donna Summer?"

"Bingo. He and Ernest were doing disco moves to 'She Works Hard for the Money.' It's a miracle I didn't wreck this damn thing. Fifteen more minutes and we're switching to the Dead."

We agreed to stop outside Diamondhead, Mississippi at a roadside park for a late lunch and I signed off.

"Funk, disco, *and* drug music?" Ruth asked with an arched eyebrow.

"Be glad we're back here and they're up there," I said.

"Don't worry," she assured me. "I am."

When we did stop, we were pleased to discover that at some point during their rolling concert tour, the guys made sandwiches. We broke out the chips and settled down to eat, not planning to linger in favor of ending the day's drive early.

While we ate, everyone multitasked.

Dex and I consulted our maps to confirm the next leg of the trip.

Ruth double-checked with the owner of the property where we'd be staying that night.

Ernest asked to see the photos Olivia took at the cemetery that morning.

Out of the corner of my eye, I saw her pull the new iPhone out of her pocket. She thumbed open the image app and started to show Ernest the shots while he hovered over her shoulder.

Dex and I were arguing about what he called a "shortcut" and I called "a swamp road from hell," when I heard Ernest say, "Who's that?"

The question didn't register as significant until Olivia didn't answer. We all fell silent one by one when we realized she'd gone deathly silent.

"What?" I asked.

All Olivia could do was hand the phone to me. Ernest supplied the explanation. "Look behind Ruth, at the edge of the woods by that pointy white gravestone."

Frowning at the screen, I put two fingers on the glass and enlarged the image.

"Oh shit," I said, shoving the phone over to Johnny. He stared for a moment, then flipped on the TV and worked some bit of techno magic to display the phone's screen on the monitor.

There, in the shadow of the deep forest, stood the figure of man. He'd been watching us the whole time we were in the cemetery and no one had sensed his presence.

But the worst part?

I recognized him: the grinning son of a bitch from the alley in San Antonio.

Right about now, you're thinking that was the bombshell revelation of the day. Wrong. Olivia had something much bigger teed up: the admission that she'd seen the guy before — in another cemetery. Where she was visiting our grandmother's grave.

Yeah. *Our.*

Maybe you saw that coming, but I sure as hell didn't.

To be fair, Olivia didn't blurt out the news about our familial relationship. She began with, "There are some things I haven't told you."

If I had a dollar for every client who made that admission through the years, I'd be set for life.

"I'm assuming he's one of those things," I said, pointing at the screen.

"Yes."

Typically that would have been my cue to go into the "if you don't tell me everything, I can't help you" lecture, but Olivia wasn't being evasive. She was visibly rattled, but also clear-eyed and resolute.

"Who is he?" I asked.

When Olivia said she didn't know, I believed her. Without prompting, she asked Johnny to put her family tree on the TV screen. The vampire tapped a few keys.

"Now," Olivia said, "show us the matrilineal line."

More key clicks.

The screen displayed two names I'd seen before: Norman and Madeline Gallo — Maddy was named for her mother. Olivia hadn't mentioned, however, that she had an aunt, Elizabeth Gallo.

Olivia kept her eyes on my face when she asked, "Does the name Elizabeth Gallo mean anything to you?"

"No. Should it?"

"Elizabeth left home at an early age; I think to get away from Madeline. The information in the child services report describes her as controlling and manipulative."

Uh, yeah. She charged her own daughter for babysitting.

"Elizabeth changed her name to Gannon."

When I went utterly still, Dex put his hand on my arm. "Selby? What is it?"

I didn't answer him. I couldn't.

Elizabeth Gannon Manners. The name carved on one side of a tombstone in Crystal City — the side covering an empty grave.

Don't think I'm cold-hearted for what I did next. Long-lost relative reunions go a lot better in the movies than they do in real life. I didn't think Olivia would lie to me, but since I had a way to prove her story, I used it.

"Johnny," I said calmly, "do you have my DNA file with you?"

The vampire frowned. "I have the ability to access the information remotely from the office server."

"Good. Could you please compare it to Olivia's and tell me what you see?"

When we first began to work together, Johnny put my genetic data on file for a grisly, but realistic reason. If any one of the supernatural creatures with whom we deal ever took me out, DNA might be the only way to identify the scraps.

The display changed. Johnny leaned forward to study the screen.

"Would one of you please tell us what's going on here?" Ruth asked.

Johnny answered before either Olivia or I could. "It would seem that Olivia and Selby are cousins. As a rough estimate of their common DNA, I would venture to suggest first cousins."

Rather than be offended by my caution; Olivia seemed relieved. The science backed up her story. "That's right," she said. "Elizabeth was Selby's mother."

At that, everyone started talking at once and kept talking until I cut them off.

"Could you all give us a minute, please?"

Dex and Ruth stepped outside. Helen blinked out. Ernest flowed into the pipes, and Johnny retreated to the bedroom at the rear of the vehicle, snagging his headphones as he went.

The vampire couldn't tone down his super bat ears, but he could use technology and music to give me and Olivia privacy. I thanked him with my eyes as he closed the sliding door.

"I'm sorry I didn't tell you sooner," Olivia said the instant we were alone. "I meant to say something and then I found out about being a dhampir. Everything started moving so fast and I liked all of you so much. I just got scared."

"Telling me we're cousins scared you more than finding out you're a dhampir?"

Olivia looked down. "I didn't know if you'd want to be related to me."

In spite of the seriousness of the moment, I laughed. "I introduced you to a witch, a vampire, a ghost, a wildfire elemental, and whatever the hell Dex is and you were worried about being a dhampir?"

My new cousin shrugged helplessly. "I know, silly, right?"

"Very," I said, reaching across the space between us and laying my hand over hers.

Olivia intertwined our fingers. We sat quietly until I said, "You look like her. Like Liz — my mother. The first time I saw you there was something familiar in your face, but I couldn't put my finger on it."

"You're the first blood relative I've met since they took my siblings away," Olivia said, the words filled with unshed tears. "You're exactly the kind of person I hoped to find when I started all this."

Oh, honey, I thought. *If you think being a dhampir is bad, wait until you find out the truth about Auntie Liz and yours truly.*

"We have a lot to talk about," I said.

Olivia nodded, but instantly showed the one family trait that has saved my butt over and over again — practicality. "We do need to talk, but we aren't safe here, are we? This place is too exposed."

"It is," I agreed, "and we need to lose your stalker. Do you have any idea what he's after?"

"Yes," Olivia said, "but I think everyone needs to see this."

26

Olivia retrieved a messenger bag from her cubicle and removed a book wrapped in clean newspaper. “This was buried at our grandparents’ grave,” she explained, laying the volume in the center of the table.

The odor of old leather and pungent earth reached my nose. “How did you know to look for it there?” I asked.

“From a dream,” she said, “or maybe a vision. I’m not sure which. The day I found it was the first time I saw the man who was in the cemetery this morning.”

To my surprise, she hadn’t opened the book yet. Seeing the man standing at the edge of the woods in Massachusetts scared her so badly, Olivia immediately purchased an airline ticket and headed for Texas. Thankfully without any awareness that he must have been right behind her.

Now we were being cautious about examining the volume because handling potentially supernatural objects should follow certain protocols. For all we knew something more than paper could be bound within the leather cover. The last thing we needed to do was release an unknown entity.

Instead, we walked Olivia through her story in detail looking for anything that might help us to make an educated guess about why the book was placed in the grave at all.

"Tell me again about the dream," I said.

"*Dreams*," Olivia corrected me. "They went on for three weeks before I figured out which cemetery to visit. In the dreams, I saw myself approaching a gravestone engraved with Norman and Madeline's names. The grass at the base of the tombstone split and a metal box rose out of the ground. When it opened, this book was lying inside."

Johnny, who was taking notes on his tablet, said, "But when you located the actual resting place it was not marked, correct?"

"That's right," Olivia said. "They're both buried in a single grave."

She went on to describe the narrator's voice in the dreamscape. Each time before awakening a woman commanded Olivia to, "Seek the book that sleeps in my grave." Olivia believed the speaker to be Madeline.

"Why do you think it was her?" I asked.

She gave me a solid, logical answer. "Norman died first. If the book had been there already, someone would have found it when they opened the plot to bury Madeline."

"True," I said, "but Madeline couldn't have put the book there herself if she was dead."

Johnny interrupted. "You do not know that," he said. "We are familiar with many beings that possess post-mortem physicality." He was looking at Dex when he said it.

I conceded the point and moved on. "Olivia, what do you know about our grandmother?" The English major in me registered the unnatural feel of the plural possessive.

There had been no time to confess to my cousin that I'd never known my maternal grandparents' names or even where they lived. Mom refused to discuss her childhood — now I better understood her motivations.

"The records are vague," she said, "but I'm pretty sure she was a gypsy who married an Italian man in Boston."

"Interesting," Johnny said, typing on the screen.

"*Interesting* as in a factor in Olivia's dhampirism?" I asked.

The vampire looked up. "Not on the face of things. In our more politically correct age the word 'gypsy' is taken to be a pejorative reference to the Roma or Romani people. Culturally they are not as films portray them. The Roma are superstitious, but they do not generally believe in curses and the like. None of that, however, rules out the possibility that Madeline was, in some way, supernaturally gifted."

"She must have been," Olivia replied. "When I dug up the box, the latch was frozen. I used my knife to force it. The blade slipped and cut my fingers. Blood fell on the cover and sizzled."

I looked over at Ruth. "Can you get a read on that?"

In response, she extended her arm, allowed her hand to hover inches over the book, and closed her eyes. After a minute she said, "Nothing but low-level energy, not enough for anyone with awareness to notice."

Before we could circle back through the facts again, Dex interrupted. "Let's get someplace safer before we go on with this."

"Agreed," I said, "but we need to find a new place to stop for the night. I'm not going to make it easy for this jerk to show up again."

Fifteen minutes later, Dex, Ruth, and I stood in the shade under a clump of trees out of earshot of The Hearse. Johnny couldn't join us for obvious reasons; Helen and Earnest wouldn't leave Olivia.

Even though Olivia and I both recognized the stalker as the same man who photobombed her camera play, back in San Antonio, I had wanted to see the images side by side.

The mystery figure appeared thin to the point of emaciation.

His sallow complexion and yellowed teeth made him look menacing and almost feral, with a manic light in his dark eyes. I can't say why, but my gut told me he'd spent time inside a jail cell. The hard set of his mouth suggested he deserved to be there.

The pictures didn't give us much to go on, but we could draw some inferences. The guy appeared in daylight, so he wasn't a vampire.

Don't believe that bullshit legend about bloodsuckers having no reflection. The undead can appear in mirrors and photographs, but with a distorted likeness. Generally the effect resembles what you'd see through a dirty, smeared glass.

The figure in Olivia's photo appeared in sharp focus even at a distance. There were no auras or telltale signs surrounding his form. Chances were good that the man was human, but we couldn't be positive. He looked like a garden variety thug, but one that got a drop on me, a powerful witch, and two ghosts.

The patchy timeline also bothered me. Olivia saw the stalker in the Massachusetts cemetery, but she had no idea how long he might have been following her prior to that day or why. Had he wanted the book all along or because he'd watched Olivia dig it up?

I recounted all of this to Don Eugenio on the phone, ending with, "We need an alternate stop for the night. You're on speaker, by the way."

"Understood," the Don replied, his voice sounding tinny through the connection. "I agree that remaining on your current course would be a mistake, although you may not be able to avoid continued surveillance. I will make calls and forward revised instructions."

The instant the connection broke I took out my frustrations on my husband — an unfair spousal privilege that I abused six ways from Sunday.

“What the *hell*, Dex?” I demanded. “You told me you wanted to be ‘on the clock’ on this one. You didn’t notice we were being tailed by some freaking graveyard stalker?”

Dex didn't take my cheap shot lying down because I could see his frustration level was as high as mine or higher.

“You were standing right there looking at the asshole in broad daylight and you didn’t see him either. Back off, Selby.”

It probably sounded like a fight, but it wasn’t. We needed to blow off steam and get our heads back in the game. Since Ruth never so much as batted an eye, she apparently understood that.

Finally Dex heaved a heavy sigh and ran a hand through his close-cropped hair. “The asshole got past us, but he didn’t get past an iPhone, which should mean he can’t dodge a bullet.”

“Good,” I said, “because the first chance I get, I’ll be happy to wing one in his direction.”

When my phone signaled the arrival of an email from Don Eugenio, I passed the device to Ruth who smiled when she saw the name of the property’s owner: Imogene Oradell MacIntosh.

"That’s a joke, right?" I asked.

"Not at all," Ruth replied. "Eugenio is sending us to coven land. When we get there, you'll understand why he chose this location. I know Mac. We can stay as long as necessary to figure out the significance of the book."

The changed itinerary called for us to backtrack to Slidell and head north on 59. At Meridian, we’d pick up 20 and make for Tuscaloosa. Our destination was a spot on the Black Warrior River near a wide place in the road called Fosters.

Dex briefly studied the map. “We need to get rolling. I don’t want us on the road after dark. You driving or riding?”

“I’d rather drive,” I said. “Better visibility, but I should run it by Olivia.”

When I climbed in the coach, my cousin was sitting on the sofa with Ernest, back in teddy bear mode, on one side and

Helen on the other. I squatted down, putting one hand on her knee.

"How you doing?"

"Better," she said, "but I'll be glad when we stop for the night."

"You want me to let somebody else drive the Jeep, so I can stay here with you?"

She shook her head. "That would drive you absolutely nuts. I'll be fine."

"We'll stay with her," Ernest said, scooting closer to Olivia. "Go on and drive, *jefe*."

Helen rolled her eyes. "How many times do I have to tell you it's *jefa* with an 'a?'"

I looked at Olivia and cocked an eyebrow. "See what I mean about us being a family? You don't just get me, you get us all."

"Thank God," she said, with tears in her eyes, "because I really need you guys."

Ruth was waiting for me outside the coach's door. We walked to the Jeep together. When I turned the key in the ignition, I said, "Changing directions makes me feel like we're doing something, but let's be honest, we're still being watched — I wish I knew by who."

"Or by *what*," Ruth added.

27

The Black Warrior River turned out to be a substantial body of water responsible for the generation of hydroelectric power throughout west and central Alabama. Or at least that's what a quick search on my phone told me when we stopped for gas in Pachuta, Mississippi.

We covered the 144 miles from Slidell without stopping. For the first half hour my eyes shifted restlessly toward the rear view mirror every few seconds until Ruth said quietly, "Relax. Save all that energy until you have something to fight. Do you want to talk about Olivia being your cousin?"

"I'm not sure everything's sunk in yet," I admitted. "It would have been nice to meet her under better circumstances, but Olivia's great. I will say it makes this dhampir business damned personal though."

"It already was," Ruth said. "You care about all your clients. That's why you're so good at what you do."

Squirming under the praise, I said, "Could we table the subject of my screwed-up family for a while? I'm one nerve cell away from overload."

"Sure," Ruth said. "Let me find something we can listen to."

She hunted around until she found a radio station playing soft, mostly aimless jazz. I willed myself to settle against the seat allowing my thoughts to play up and down the scales with the music for a mile or two before I said, "This probably isn't fair since I don't want to talk about the complicated crap in my past, but that was a hell of a story you told us about your father last night."

"I don't mind," Ruth replied. "Hell is a good word to associate with my father. I told that story because I wanted Olivia — and you — to know you aren't alone in weighing your humanity against your differences."

The generosity of the answer didn't surprise me; the self-doubt did. I thought Ruth left those internal questions behind when she walked out of the girl's school for the last time.

When I asked her about it, she said, "I know who and what I am now, but there are things about Olivia that remind me of myself at that age."

To my eye it would be difficult to imagine two women more different than Ruth Beauchene and Olivia Reynolds. Even with her gentle, stable demeanor, there's always a suggestion of something exotic about Ruth, a quality I saw at the time as being absent in Olivia.

"What were you doing when you were 36?" I asked.

Ruth considered the question. "I'd just finished my master's degree," she said. "I had a job in the public-school system by day."

Well, that was an opening a mile wide.

"And by night?"

Someone else might have dodged the question, but Ruth owned up to her youthful indiscretions.

"Dating one in a series of Mr. Inappropriates whose names I don't even remember. That was the last stage of my rebellious

Cajun streak. Straight-laced school marm by day, roadhouse babe by night."

The series of revelations made focusing on the road difficult. "Don't get me wrong," I said. "I have no doubt you turned heads then because you turn them now, but it's hard for me to imagine you as a wild child."

"Thank God," Ruth said. "I made a concerted effort to start growing up after I hit 40. As a younger woman I didn't have much of a sense of purpose. All that bad behavior was driven by the kind of confusion Olivia is experiencing. In my case, at least, that included a heavy dose of self-loathing courtesy of my father's small-minded condemnation. I feel for her."

Ruth's admission made me think about the story of the man who, when shown all the problems endured by others, chooses to keep his own and quit complaining.

Life handed me a supernatural infection created by my mother's bad choices. Ruth endured a drunken father who regarded her as the spawn of the devil. Olivia faced abandonment, chronic illness, and now an identity that placed her square in the middle of a paranormal political mess.

The trick isn't trading your problems for someone else's; it's playing the hand you're dealt and making the most of it. Maybe fate brought me and Olivia together to accomplish that very thing.

When we made that stop for gas in Pachuta, I climbed into the coach to have a word with Helen and to check on my cousin. I found the sliding doors to Olivia's tiny cubicle pulled shut.

"How long has she been in there?" I asked Helen, keeping my voice low.

"Since we left the rest area," Helen said. "I blipped in one time to check on her. She was asleep, or at least pretending to be."

From the area of the kitchen, Ernest flowed out of one of the stove burners. "You want me to slide in there and keep an eye on her, Boss Lady?"

I considered the offer but told him no. I understood that Olivia needed time to process. Hell, I needed the same thing, but that luxury wasn't going to be a line item on my schedule any time in the foreseeable future.

Three hours and one more gas stop later, I maneuvered the Jeep down a private road, hanging back to avoid eating any more of The Hearse's dust than necessary.

The sun had started to sink toward the horizon. Through the heavy tree cover on our right I caught glimpses of light glinting off a broad, calm stream I assumed was the Black Warrior.

After a mile and a half, we pulled to a stop in front of a white, two-story farmhouse with a gracious front porch complete with rocking chairs. The whole place looked like it had been plucked off a greeting card.

When Ruth described the property as "coven land," I half expected a welcoming committee comprised of thirteen black-clad women with pointy hats.

Instead, a roundish woman bounced out of the house. The screen slammed shut behind her. She wore fuchsia polyester pants and a matching sweatshirt covered by a bright green apron emblazoned with the words, "I'd Give You the Recipe, But Then I'd Have to Kill You."

"Mary Ruth *Beauchene*!" she trilled, flapping one ring-bedecked hand in the direction of the Jeep. "*Sugar!* You get out here and give me a hug right this *instant!*"

Ignoring her Southern double name with good-natured forbearance, Ruth climbed out and allowed herself to be engulfed in a motherly embrace.

No sooner had our hostess turned Ruth loose than she trained her sights on me.

"And *you* must be Selby!" the woman gushed, waving me out of the Jeep. "Get on over here and give me a hug, too."

Normally, I'm not much for the whole public displays of affection thing, but there was something infectious and irrepressible about this woman's hospitality. Well, that and whether I would have owned up to it or not, I needed a hug.

The moment my boots hit the ground, I understood why Eugenio sent us here. A buzz of magical current coursed up my legs. It reminded me of the warding spell that protects a secluded patch of land I own in Texas.

The white witch who cast the spell for me did such a good job that when I'm there, I blip off the supernatural radar. Not even Helen, who is bound to me by the combined energies of life and death, can pick up my "signal."

Our hostess stood on tiptoe to lace her arms around my neck. I stooped to make up for the difference in our height and hugged back as the woman introduced herself.

"I'm Imogene Oradell MacIntosh, but everybody round these parts calls me Mac. Which is a blessing. I do not *know* what my Mama was *thinking* picking out a name for me like Imogene Oradell. Sounds like a fatal diagnosis, don't it?"

In spite of everything, I laughed and agreed. "Yes, ma'am. Thank you for letting us camp on your land tonight on such short notice."

"Oh," Mac said merrily, "this place isn't mine. It belongs to the coven. When Don Eugenio called, the girls were tickled to let you all stay, especially when they heard Ruth was with you. We all just loved Genevieve. We wanted to do a potluck, but Eugenio explained you've got yourself a vampire/stalker problem. Once you get that cleared up, you have to promise you'll come back."

Blinking under the torrent of words, I managed another,

"Yes, ma'am," as I caught a glimpse of Ruth laughing silently behind Mac.

By this time, Dex and Olivia had stepped out of the Hearse, but Helen was nowhere in sight.

Mac crinkled her eyes in the direction of the RV and said, "Now, come on little ghost gal. You don't have to go hiding yourself from me. That goes for the vampire driving that big old thing, too. Lord have mercy, I bet it costs you all the earth to fill that bus up."

Helen materialized and gave Mac a shy wave as the woman trained her attention on Dex. "Huh," she said, "you I can't quite figure out."

That made two of us.

"I get that a lot," he replied. "I'm Dex Jensen, Selby's husband. It's a pleasure to meet you, Mac."

When he greeted the woman, he flashed her that killer grin and instantly had Mac eating out of the palm of his hand.

Johnny introduced himself next, bending low to kiss the back of Mac's knuckles, a gesture which made her giggle with pleasure.

A transformed version of Olivia appeared behind Johnny, revived by the setting of the sun. No longer, pale and tired, she looked energized and completely engaged — so much so that she had her messenger bag slung over one shoulder. I knew the book from the graveyard was inside. Good thinking, cousin. Good thinking.

When Mac extended her hands and moved to greet Olivia, a warm wind swept over the yard. "Welcome to my home, sweetheart," Mac said gently. "Nothing's gonna hurt you while you're on this land or try to take what's yours."

Whatever Olivia expected, that wasn't it. On impulse, she reached for the older woman. Maybe Mac used magic when they embraced. Maybe she simply called on the natural enchantment of a loving heart. It doesn't matter.

Strengthened by the disappearance of the sun or not, Olivia craved the comfort Mac offered.

When they parted, Mac kept hold of Olivia's hand as she directed Dex and Johnny about parking the coach under a nearby copse of trees.

"Then you all get yourselves back on up to the house," she commanded with good-natured authority. "I started cooking soon as I got off the phone with Eugenio. Come round to the kitchen door and let yourselves in."

"I'll park the Jeep and come back with the guys," I said.

"Suit yourself," Mac replied. "Don't forget to bring the wildfire elemental with you. Everybody's welcome here. I cook on a wood stove. He can play in the coals while we eat."

That's all it took for Ernest to explode out of the tailpipe. "Hey, Witch Lady? Do I have to wait, or can I come now?"

Mac, who was ushering Olivia and Ruth toward the house, called back, "Come ahead, but don't you go getting soot on my curtains and no sparks in the house."

"Yes, ma'am," Ernest said, shooting past me like a charcoal rocket. "I promise."

28

After we parked the vehicles, Dex, Johnny, and I started across the field toward the house. The deepening twilight felt soothing; the conversation did not. We talked about the need to keep watch through the night and debated whether we should have left the coach unattended. Johnny assured us the vehicle's onboard motion sensors would trigger an alarm if anyone tried to get in.

Since he would be up all night anyway, Johnny volunteered to stay close to The Hearse but out of sight when we returned from dinner. Dex planned to find a vantage point where he could surveil a broader area. Helen and Ernest had already appointed themselves as Olivia's personal guardians, which left me and Ruth to divide the night in two-hour shifts.

After Ruth joined the team, I told her she needed to learn to shoot and invited her to the gun range for lessons. She played along, listening to me talk about the virtues of this or that pistol with apparent interest. Once on the firing line, however, the supposedly prim schoolmarm took my Glock and squeezed off ten fast, accurate rounds leaving a pattern on the target that scored better than mine.

Handing the weapon back to me, Ruth said, "It has a sweet trigger, but I like the weight on a Smith & Wesson better." Between magic and marksmanship, Ruth is a good witch to have around in a fight. I had zero issues with her watching my back.

I expected Olivia would protest that she, too, could take her turn on duty, but that wasn't happening — not with a massive target of a different kind on her back.

On our way to Alabama, Ruth and I discussed whether or not we should examine the book in Mac's presence. We agreed to play the situation by ear, but I was leaning in favor of including the eccentric witch in our deliberations.

The land over which we walked had more magical wards than Hogwarts. The level of expertise behind those enchantments could be a huge advantage in understanding the book's secrets.

As Dex, Johnny, and I stepped into the kitchen, Mac said, "There you are! I was about to send a search party. I hope you all don't mind eating in here. I probably should have been formal and set all this up in the dining room, but everybody always winds up in the kitchen anyway. Now you all get a plate and help yourselves. There's plenty."

"Plenty" apparently means something different in the Deep South than in the rest of the nation. We had our choice of fried chicken, ham, and pot roast along with mashed potatoes, potato salad, coleslaw, red beans, green bean casserole, carrots, homemade bread, and a whole separate table full of pies and cakes.

I almost choked when Mac said she wished she'd had more time to cook "a proper meal."

When we were seated, she asked who would like to offer the blessing. Without thinking, Olivia blurted out, "Witches say grace?"

Mac reached over and patted the back of her hand. "Sure we do, sugar. Everybody in this room is part of God's plan. Don't you be worried about that. Dex, why don't you give thanks for us?"

Slipping my hand into my husband's, I bowed my head as Dex's deep voice began, "Lord, bless this food to the nourishment of our bodies . . . "

It was hardly the first time I'd held Dex's hand or listened to him say grace. When we used to go to his Aunt Marion's for Sunday dinner she'd always ask him to offer the blessing.

This time, however, his words filled me with an unexpected sense of protection over and above anything the magic wards on the property offered. It took me a minute to figure out why. For the first time in my life, and somewhat to my surprise, I actually believed God might be listening.

Between Dex coming back from the other side, the resurfacing of my mother's cursed magic, and Olivia's unexpected appearance, the idea began to gnaw at me that maybe I wasn't totally in charge of my destiny after all. The need to believe in something larger and hopefully benevolent in the Universe had begun to soften my ironclad agnosticism.

At the word "amen," Mac touched off a round of pass the plate. Our hostess thoughtfully set a place for Helen at the table. My ghostly bestie watched the food moving by with an equanimity I know she didn't feel. In life, she'd been a chow hound, constantly fighting to keep the cheese enchiladas from going to her hips.

The morning after the car accident that killed her, when I was sleeping in Maria's guest bedroom and dealing with all of Helen's wailing relatives, my newly ectoplasmic buddy appraised her reflection in the mirror and said, "Thank God I died at my goal weight."

The group around Mac's table laughed and talked like people who didn't have a care in the world beyond wrestling over the last biscuit. Ruth and I helped clear the plates while the others hit the dessert selection.

Back at the table, Mac shoveled a diabetes-inducing load of sugar into her cup and said brightly, "So! You all want to talk about the book in Olivia's bag now?"

I cocked an eyebrow in my cousin's direction. "You told her about the book without discussing it with us first?"

The words came out sharper than I intended, eliciting a defensive reaction from Olivia. "I didn't tell her anything!"

"Quit your fussing," Mac scolded. "You can't bring something like that book into a witch's house and expect her not to feel it."

"Feel what?" Ruth asked. "When I tried to get a read on the book I didn't detect anything but low-level energy."

"Of course you didn't," Mac replied. "The book knew you all weren't someplace safe. Soon as Olivia walked through the front door, I felt the magic start to sing. Listen, you'll see what I mean."

Ruth closed her eyes and cocked her head searching for something my ears would never hear. "A violin?" she said finally.

"A *gypsy* violin," Mac said. "Put the book on the table, honey."

Olivia opened the messenger bag and pulled out the book, pushing aside her dessert plate with a half-eaten slice of pecan pie to make room.

I'm sure you expected salt circles or burning candles for this part, but the first magic was that of the hearth and cook fire. We'd shared a good meal. Laughed. Embraced each other's differences. There was more than enough spontaneous protection in the room to keep us safe.

"Untie the strap," Mac commanded.

Olivia hesitated. "Shouldn't you be the one to do it?"

"Nobody showed up in *my* dreams telling me to go digging

in a graveyard," the witch said. "You were meant to find the book. It's okay. Open it."

Her fingers shook slightly, but Olivia grasped the end of the cord and pulled. The strap had only been looped over itself, not tied in a knot, so the leather came away easily. The book fell open — with no help from Olivia — as the pages fluttered to a spot mid-way through the volume and stopped.

Talk about an anti-climax; the paper was completely blank.

"That's a buzz kill," Helen said. "Are we supposed to write something?"

Mac pushed her chair away and stood. "Let's go in the parlor. Bring the book, honey."

We trailed after her, Olivia balancing the open book in her outstretched hands.

"Come over here by the piano," Mac instructed. The word came out "pie-annie" in her thick Southernese.

She sat down in front of the instrument, a hulking, black upright and closed her eyes. Humming along with music none of us but Ruth could follow, Mac's fingers played a series of notes on the yellowed keys that I took to be the end of a musical phrase.

A phrase that also functioned as a trigger. When the last note sounded, ink flowed from the book's spine forming lines of tight, cramped handwriting.

My oldest child has become enamored of a man not wholly of this world. Impure blood flows through his veins and will taint the children born to them. I have forbidden Maddie to bring the unclean spirit into my home.

A black line slashed across the page separating the first entry from the next. Similar lines marked both pages creating a series of truncated diary entries recording the births of Olivia and her siblings.

> *Maddie's husband abandoned her and the children. She wants my help. I agreed to watch the brats, but only to study them. I'm forcing her to pay me for the time I spend with the creatures. I won't let Satan into my house through the open door of affection.*

Brats? Creatures? So *not* Grandma of the Year material.

The combined entries told us that somehow Madeline sensed Vinnie possessed vampire blood. She tried to find out more about his background, uncovering a prior marriage in the process.

A single line comprised the final entry: *"His first-born harbors the greatest evil."*

When Olivia tried to turn the page, the book snapped shut,

"That's it?" I said. "Who the hell is the first born?"

"I don't know," Mac replied. "The book isn't singing now. It doesn't have anything else to say for the time being."

"Too damn bad," I said heatedly. "Give it a kick and wake it up again."

Ruth laid a hand on my arm. "You know magic doesn't work like that. We're all tired. We need to get some rest."

"She's right," Dex said. "We can work on this 'first born' business in the morning. Everybody's had enough for one day."

The plan went against the grain, but I gave in. Dex and Johnny insisted on going back to the coach first to check for intruders. The rest of us waited on the porch for the agreed upon signal: three bursts from Dex's flashlight.

When I saw the all clear, I stood up and said, "Time to go."

"Are you sure I can't convince you all to stay up here at the house tonight?" Mac asked.

"Afraid not," I replied. "The coach is easier to guard, and we don't want to put you in any danger."

The old woman made a scoffing sound. "Nothing can hurt me on this land."

Ernest stirred in the shadows beside me. "I hope you're right about that Witch Lady, 'cause we've got company."

The moon broke from behind the clouds and illuminated a lone figure in the middle of the field. All the sounds of the night fell silent as a sing-song voice called out, "Red Rover, Red Rover, send Baby Sister right over."

29

Olivia took one step before I stopped her. "Forget it. Not happening."

She started to argue with me, but Mac put an arm around her shoulders. "You come on in the house with me," the witch said quietly but firmly. "Your time to step up is coming, but not tonight."

When the screen door closed, I turned to Ruth, "Whatever happens, don't let Olivia out of this house."

"Understood," she said. "Are you sure you want to deal with this situation without any backup?"

In the tension of the moment I mentally paused long enough to be grateful Ruth didn't ask what I was going to do or argue with me about it. We'd faced circumstances like this together in the past — and I suspect we will in the future. Ruth conserves her energies for the time when they'll do the most good. Arguing with me there on the porch wasn't one of those times.

"There's no way Dex didn't hear this asshole," I said. "I'll have backup."

Helen floated closer. "I'll make sure of that. Anything you want me to tell Dex?"

"Yeah," I said, "tell him I want that guy alive long enough for him to answer some questions."

She blipped out as Ernest roiled in the darkness near the door. "What about me?"

"Stay here with Ruth."

The night we took down the Shadow Man, the witch and the elemental proved to be an unlikely but effective duo. The experience created a bond of trust between them I knew they'd instinctively rely on if things took a bad turn.

Unholstering my gun, I started down the walk keeping my eyes on the figure in the field. With my attention trained on the intruder, I didn't feel the forces in the land under my feet until I'd almost reached him. Then my skin began to crawl.

Shit, shit, *shit*. Not now. Please God if you are there, not now.

When the violet light reached my eyes I saw them. Hundreds of glowing creatures swarming through the field and converging on me, their life force calling to the curse infecting my body. The blood in my veins burned like lava as my muscles and bones strained to expand and contort.

"Hurts like hell, don't it?" the man said, grinning that same demonic grin from the photos. "Let it take you, Cousin Selby. You'll feel better when you shift."

Fighting to keep my gun level, I said, "Who the hell are you?"

"Why, don't you recognize your own kinfolk?" he asked. "I'm Vinnie's oldest boy, Lonnie. The Judge and me been waiting a long time for another one to wake up. Now you be a good lil birdie and get Olivia on out here so we can all go back to Wrightsville together."

Through clenched teeth I made an anatomically impossible suggestion about what he could do with that idea.

"Granddaddy said you'd be like that," Lonnie said. "Liz didn't want to work with us either, least wise not until we arranged for her to get some real power. First taste of blood got her in the family business quick enough though. She's looking forward to seeing you again, by the way. Don't you go holding it against her that she had to tear your Daddy up like that. He was what you call collateral damage."

That got him a bullet in the gut. One that should have put him down for the count. Instead, Lonnie looked at the blood-stained, greasy plaid covering his belly, and said, "Now why'd you have to go and do that? This is my favorite shirt."

I struggled to fire again, but the shaking in my limbs made it impossible to aim. Rustling footsteps sounded behind me. For a panicked moment I thought Olivia had followed me into the field, but then Ruth touched my arm.

I don't know what she saw when our eyes met — I didn't want to know. She hesitated for a fraction of a second and then her grip tightened. "Resist it," she said. "Don't let it take over."

My vision swam crazily, but I managed to croak. "Not. Safe. Get back."

Lonnie made an impatient, scoffing sound. "This is taking too much time."

When he moved toward us, Ruth's hand shot out, throwing him back on a wave of billowing power. "Stay where you are," she warned, keeping hold of me. "I won't be so gentle next time."

Even in my altered state, I heard the dangerous edge in Lonnie's voice. "You bitch, you shouldn't have done that."

If Ruth hadn't been preoccupied with me, Lonnie never would have gotten the drop on her. A shot rang out. Ruth's touch fell away as she crumpled to the ground. The last threads of my sanity went with her.

My nostrils flared at the scent of the blood pumping from her shoulder. I felt thick heat rising from the viscous liquid and listened to the rapid, pained thumping of her heart. A terrible ravenous hunger consumed me, urging me to do the unthinkable — sink my claws into my friend's flesh and rip her open so I could feed.

On the ragged fringes of my diminishing awareness, Lonnie goaded me. "Go on. Do it."

Reeling back, I fell to my knees and willed my hand to bring the gun to my temple. I felt the cold metal of the barrel against my skin, but then a strong hand took the weapon from me.

A second man was in the field. A man who wasn't Dex.

I heard Lonnie snarl, "What the fuck are you doing? You work for us."

"Not anymore I don't," a voice answered. A flash split the darkness — a flash from Hunt Walker's old Peacemaker.

THE FIRST LIGHT of dawn coming through lace curtains awakened me. As I tried to sit up, I recognized the touch of Dex's hand. "Easy, baby. Not so fast."

My body ached like I'd taken a beating and my throat burned. With Dex's support, I sipped a glass of water. The cool liquid felt heavenly going down.

"Ruth?" I croaked as he eased me back onto the pillow.

"In the next bedroom," Dex said. "Johnny's with her. The shot was a through and through. She'll be fine."

"Olivia?"

"Worried out of her mind about you, but safe."

"Lonnie?"

Dex's jaw tightened. "Dead."

"Who killed him?"

A rumbling voice off to my left said, "I did."

Dex didn't look like he wanted to do it, but he gestured the speaker into the room. "I take it you two know each other?" he said.

Blinking to keep my eyes open, I recognized Hunt Walker. "You're the guy from Luther's gun range," I mumbled. "What the hell are you doing here?"

"That's a long story," Hunt said, "one you can't stay awake for. We'll talk when you've rested."

For three days I drifted in and out. Sometimes I had an awareness that Dex was with me, and sometimes Helen was there. When I did come fully conscious, however, the first thing I saw was my husband's face, covered in heavy stubble.

When I tugged at his shirt sleeve and said, "You need a shave and I'm hungry," he gave me the most relieved smile I've ever seen on his face, but tears filled his eyes.

Overachiever that I am, I scared the hell out of everybody.

With Dex's help, I dressed and went downstairs, sending Mac into a fit of motherly ministrations. My focus, however, was on Ruth who was lying on the sofa in the parlor. Her face was drawn, but her eyes were clear.

Johnny vacated his chair at her side so I could sit with her, but not before kissing me on the cheek and murmuring, "Dear Selby, thank God you are unharmed."

I reached for Ruth's hand, pleased at the strength with which she squeezed my fingers. "You look like hell," I said.

"Have you looked in a mirror?" she asked.

"From now on," I said, my voice cracking, "you're carrying a gun. No arguments."

Her grip tightened. "You sound like Johnny."

Swallowing against the lump in my throat, I said, "For once, Johnny's right."

Behind me, the vampire said, "*Sacré Dieu*, perhaps you have suffered permanent damage after all, dear Selby."

Everyone laughed, but Ruth and I held each other's gaze. We

knew how close I'd come to losing a battle in that field that had nothing to do with Lonnie.

Approaching footsteps crossed the hardwood. I turned to see Olivia enter the room with a steaming mug in her hand. She managed to set it on the coffee table before engulfing me in a bear hug; her body trembled in my arms.

"It's okay," I said against her ear. "I'm fine. Really."

My cousin pulled away, wiping her eyes. "Mac told me to bring you this tea. I don't know what's in it, but she said it will make you feel better."

Sniffing experimentally at the liquid, I smelled bourbon. Mac was definitely my kind of nurse.

Hunt appeared in the door next. I hadn't noticed before, but he was sporting a major shiner. "Who gave you that?" I asked, sipping the hot toddy.

"Your husband," he replied, leaning against the doorframe. "Bastard packs a mean right."

Dex shifted uncomfortably. "I didn't know if he was on our side or not. Ruth had a bullet in her, you . . . weren't yourself, and this guy was standing over a dead man with a smoking .45 in his hand. What was I supposed to do?"

"Hold it," I said. ""Could somebody please start at the beginning and tell me the whole story? I don't remember anything after Hunt took my gun away."

My husband's face registered shock. "You let someone take your gun?"

How was I supposed to tell Dex how close I came to putting a bullet in my brain? God love her, Ruth did it for me.

"Selby was trying to stop the transformation the only way she knew how."

The room fell silent. When he got past the initial shock of the statement, Dex stood up and walked over to Hunt. Holding out his hand, Dex said, "Thank you. I owe you for that."

After they shook, Johnny said, "Perhaps it would be best if I narrated the series of events."

"Yeah," I agreed. "Good plan. Go for it."

While the vampire talked, I drank my bourbon-laced tea, ate the heaping plate of bacon and eggs Mac served to me on a tray, and kept an eye on my husband's ashen face. Dex knew me better than anyone in the room. If Hunt hadn't stopped me, I would have pulled the trigger.

Johnny began with the parts I remembered. He and Dex went to the coach and flashed us the all clear. They heard Lonnie's taunting call and tried to come into the field only to be stopped by the same glowing beings that converged on me.

The entities affected Helen as well. She got stuck over the field, forced to watch what was happening, but unable to do anything to help.

Mac interrupted at that point to explain that the creatures were the guardians of the land. We mistook the reclusive river elementals for warding magic.

Red undulations I recognized as embarrassment washed through Ernest as he floated next to Olivia on a settee near the piano.

"Sorry, Boss Lady. I didn't get a read on them. You know, fire/water? Not the greatest match. Totally my bad. But when I recognized what they were, I got them to listen to me so Ruth could come out and try to help you."

"The elementals were attracted to Selby's shifter magic," Mac said apologetically. "They didn't mean to hurt you."

Everyone in the room saw what happened to me that night. Going back in the supernatural closet wasn't an option.

"Something attacked me when I was a teenager," I said. "It's a long story. I'll tell you later. Right now, I need to know, did I change?"

"No," Ruth assured me. "You came close, but you never

shifted. It wasn't your fault. Lonnie was carrying a charm that triggered the shift to begin."

Wonder who helped him come up with that? Oh, wait. Yeah! My mother, the murdering bird witch.

I looked over at Hunt. "What's your story?"

"Malachi Reeves has had me working undercover for The Judge in Wrightsville for the past few months," he said. "We knew he and Lonnie were up to something, but we didn't know the specifics until Lonnie started tailing Olivia. Before you get riled up, Don Eugenio didn't know anything about it. Believe me, he's pissed enough for both of you."

Like that was going to stop my temper from flaring.

"Bullshit. You were in San Antonio. Six blocks from my goddamned office. You couldn't stroll on over, come clean, and save us a metric ass ton of trouble?"

Completely unfazed, Hunt said, "Nope. You weren't paying my salary. Malachi wanted to make sure Olivia wasn't hiding the location of her siblings with Don Eugenio's help. The Don's not part of the vampire nation."

"He's been an ally of the vampire nation for centuries and you damn well know it."

Hunt shrugged. "Even allies have ambitions. We had to make sure we could trust all of you. This thing is a lot bigger than you realize."

Even though I was expecting him to say something like that, the words still sent a chill through me. "How much bigger?"

Crossing his arms over his chest, Hunt said, "Well, for starters, Olivia thought she was the oldest of four. Turns out she's the middle child of nine. Correction, eight now that Lonnie's out of the picture."

Eight potential dhampirs?

I looked over at Mac. "Could I get another cup of your special tea?"

EPILOGUE

From there, the conversation devolved into an epic clash of opinions. Olivia wanted to push on to Wrightsville and confront the Judge. A suggestion Hunt and Dex shot down instantly, with Johnny's support.

Worry lines etched the handsome vampire's face. His eyes never strayed far from Ruth. "We must return to our home base and regroup," he said, "not charge into the Russian winter like Napoleon."

The reference got him a round of blank stares until Ruth said, "Napoleon invaded Russia without adequate resources to survive the winter. Johnny's trying to say we're in no shape to go on. I hate to do this, Selby, but I agree. Lonnie knew how to trigger your shift. We can't go near Wrightsville, especially if your mother is there. Until I understand the magic that transformed her and infected you, I can't promise you that I can stop the shift."

Helen, who had been hovering cross-legged above the parlor door for the entire conversation, floated down in front of me. "Ruth is right. We have to figure out how to protect you before we do anything else. That's what *abuelita* would say."

"Excuse me," I said, "but am I the only one who heard the part about there being *eight* more dhampirs out there?"

"*Potential* dhampirs," Hunt said. "Lonnie and Olivia are the only two the Judge knows about. Olivia will be safer in Don Eugenio's territory until we decide our next move."

"*We*?" I said. "You're sticking around?"

Hunt couldn't help grinning when he answered me. "After Don Eugenio quit cussing Malachi in Spanish, they came to an agreement. I've got a new assignment. Human liaison from the vampire nation to Don Eugenio. Think of it as a diplomatic posting."

From what I'd seen already, Hunt Walker and I shared an equal lack of diplomatic qualities; an opinion confirmed by the dark glower on Dex's face.

Great. Just what I wanted to deal with — two posturing males.

Like Olivia, I wanted to push on to Wrightsville. Putting off a fight has never been my default position. Ruth's argument convinced me to back down. Mommie Dearest and I have unfinished business, but for the time being, she has the advantage over me — one only distance will negate.

So we came home, living to fight another day with bigger, badder weapons if I have anything to say about it. By the next morning, I felt well enough to get behind the wheel of the Jeep.

Johnny wanted Ruth in the coach so he could keep an eye on her, but she insisted on riding with me, confiding in a whisper, "He is driving me *insane*. Who knew he would turn out to be a helicopter vampire?"

In the short term, the hovering attentions might have gotten on her nerves, but Johnny's tender care and genuine distress over Ruth's injury has those two back on track as a couple. That makes me happy.

Dex and I are doing okay. That last night in Alabama when

we'd gone upstairs to go to bed, he pulled me into a fierce hug and said, "Don't you ever even *think* about hurting yourself again."

Of course I said I wouldn't, but neither will I allow myself to turn into what I saw my mother become. Dex knows it, too, which is why *he* tracks *me* with worried eyes now.

Hunt waited to brief us fully until we were back in San Antonio and seated around Don Eugenio's conference table. He had a lot to say, but I'll cut to the chase.

The Judge, also known as Seumas Stiùbhart, hasn't located the rest of his dhampir grandchildren. That buys us some time. Likely not much, but we'll take what we can get.

Luther was right to worry that there's a war coming — there is and it looks like we're going to be in it whether we want to be or not.

The experience in Alabama changed Olivia. That day at Don Eugenio's she asked the Don and Johnny to train her to enter our profession full time.

That part I didn't mind; what she wants to do with her training was a harder pill to swallow. She plans to find her siblings and either get them on our side or get them out of the game.

"It's my responsibility," she insisted. "Madeline wanted *me* to have the book."

Both Mac and Ruth agree the book has more to say, but only when it's ready. Teaching Olivia to hear the book's music and trigger future messages will be Ruth's job.

Olivia and I have spent a lot of time getting to know each other. I underestimated her in the beginning and now I fear where her true courage will lead her. I'm not thrilled about letting her go out there hunting dhampirs, but neither will I stand in the way of her calling. For now, she's with us, and no one will let her leave until she's ready.

The same can be said for me. Under Ruth's tutelage, I'm gaining better control of the shifter magic infecting my system, but I'm a long way from graduating with honors.

We have the charm Lonnie used, safely contained in salt at Ruth's house where she can study it without endangering me. Hopefully that project will allow her to develop a countermeasure.

Since our primary allegiance is to Don Eugenio, we're taking care of business here until trouble comes to our doorstep, which it will.

You remember how I bitched about that goat exorcism? Man, trot out the demonic barbecue on the hoof. It's looking good compared to what's headed our way.

A WORD FROM JULIETTE

Thank you for reading *Blood Marked*, the second Selby Jensen Paranormal Mystery. If you missed the first installment in the series, click the link to get your copy of *Descendants of the Rose* on Amazon.

> Selby Jensen's business card reads "Private Investigator," but that seriously downplays her occupation. Let's hear it in her own words:
>
> "You want to know what I do for a living? I rip souls out. Cut heads off. Put silver bullets where silver bullets need putting. You think there aren't any monsters? . . . I have some disturbing news for you. You might want to sit down. Monsters walk among us. I'm looking for one in particular. In the meantime? I'm keeping the rest of them from eating people like you."

For readers new to my novels, let me tell you about the Jinx Hamilton series, which begins with *Witch at Heart*. These books are lighter than Selby's world, but full of the same mix of paranormal and fantasy elements my readers love.

> Fresh off a long stint as a waitress, Jinx inherits her eccentric aunt's shop in Briar Hollow, North Carolina. She's immediately confronted with an enchanted inventory, an unruly clientele, and magical powers that don't come with an instruction manual!

From there, the series arc grows in complexity over a page-turning series of urban fantasy novels that take Jinx, the crew, and the reader into new adventures and even new realms.

The next story, *Witch at Odds*, puts Jinx in the awkward position of learning the consequence of getting too brave with her magic, too soon.

In *Witch at Last*, she discovers the true story behind the gift of her powers, as well as the significance of the store itself and what lies beyond.

You can buy each of these books individually, or save money with the *Six-Book Box Set*, which also contains *Witch on First*, *Witch on Second*, and *Witch on Third*.

Still not certain you want to take this journey with Jinx? I've included the first chapter of *Witch at Heart* to give you a sneak peak into Jinx's world.

The mystery, adventure, hijinks, and fun are just getting started!

Witch at Heart

Witch at Odds

Witch at Last

The Jinx Hamilton Six-Book Box Set

BUT FIRST . . . GET EXCLUSIVE MATERIAL

There are many things I love about being an author, but building a relationship with my readers is far and away the best.

Once a month I send out a newsletter with information on new releases, sneak peeks, and inside articles on all my books and series.

You can get all this, a **FREE** copy of the Jinx Hamilton prequel novella *Granny Witch*, (and more) by signing up at www.julietteharper.com.

WITCH AT HEART - SNEAK PEEK

You've heard that old saying, "Be careful what you ask for, little girl, you may get it." Well, I am living proof that sometimes, old saws can be pretty cutting edge. I said all I wanted to do was work at home and have as many cats as I could take care of. Maybe it was wish fulfillment or karma smacking me in the backside, but I am now single, 29, and the unpaid servant to four well-fed felines. We all live in the apartment above the store I inherited from my Crazy Aunt Fiona. No. Seriously. That's what we called her. Crazy Aunt Fiona.

I can see my mother now, handing me the receiver of the kitchen telephone, the one with the cord that was stretched out so straight you could wander over half the house with it. "Norma Jean, get in here and talk to your Crazy Aunt Fiona."

Yes, you read that right. Norma Jean. Mom is absolutely in love with Marilyn Monroe and chose to punish me with her obsession. Thank God Daddy heard that and said, "Lord God, woman, you have jinxed this child for life." That's the name that stuck. Jinx. Most people don't even know my real name.

Mine was a pretty conventional Southern Baptist raising in our tiny town. Mom is the devout one, and dad and me just try to stay out of trouble. By the time I made high school, I understood that we are actually "dancing Baptists." Come Sunday morning a certain brand of amnesia kicks in about where the family might have been the night before and how much country music could have been involved in the activity.

Crazy Aunt Fiona lived one town over and ran what mom referred to as a "rat's nest of a tourist trap." I could never figure out the second part of that statement since there wasn't much in our neck of the woods to see. That was before I understood some people live all their lives cooped up in cities and can't wait to enjoy some real countryside.

The other part, about the rat's nest, was a no-brainer. Dad swore a guy could walk in off the street and say, "Excuse me, do you have a spark plug for a Studebaker?" and Fiona would have produced one. She sold everything from penny candy at the counter to love potions out the back door. You want a Moon Pie and some fishing worms? Fiona had it.

The idea of a coherent inventory or any particular purpose for her store never seemed to enter her head. When she decided she wanted to serve food and the health board got all bent out of shape, Fiona just happily took the required state course, met their standards for food preparation and went right on about her business -- that is as long as the food inspector wasn't in sight.

"Everybody that comes in this place drinks homemade whiskey and would cook up road kill if it looked fresh enough," Fiona declared. "They're not gonna be catching any bubonic plague germs from me."

Truth be told, lots of folks came to Fiona to heal up from whatever was ailing them at the time. One summer I was sitting on the stool behind the counter at the store when a woman came in who had just buried her husband. She and Fiona stepped off to one side and I heard the woman say,

"Mrs. Ryan, my heart hurts so bad without Jesse I just can't breathe."

Aunt Fiona disappeared in the back of the store and came out with a piece of rose quartz on a silver chain. She said, "Now, honey, you just wear this over your heart so the magic can help you start healing. You get to thinking you can't breathe, you hold onto this piece of quartz and you pray to Jesus."

After the woman left, I said, "Aunt Fiona, how can a rock make that lady feel better about her dead husband?"

Aunt Fiona reached over and tucked my long hair behind my ears and patted my cheek with her ring-bedecked, blue-veined hand. "It's not the rock that will heal her honey, it's the belief that she *can* heal."

When Aunt Fiona would talk like that, I always felt like she was telling me things that were deep and wise because they were also simple and loving. People said Aunt Fiona was a witch woman, but the only spells I ever saw her cast were good common sense and a lot of love.

When she passed on, I was still working the same job I got the week after I graduated high school, waiting tables down at Tom's Cafe. It wasn't a bad job. I made enough to feed my cats first, and myself with what was left over. I got to see everybody in town pretty much every day and the men only made half-hearted passes at me for the fun of it. Nobody was really trying to hassle me.

The longer I worked there and the more cats I collected, the more mom clucked and said if I wasn't careful I was going to wind up a "touched" old spinster just like Aunt Fiona. Then Fiona up and died and I got called into old Judge Baker's office where I learned that I inherited Fiona's shop and a pretty nice little sum of money.

My mother had a fit, but I moved my cats and myself right on over to Briar Hollow and set myself up in Aunt Fiona's shop. I figured once I got there, I'd learn how to run the place. I mean, honestly, if I just kept stocking the same stuff Aunt Fiona put out and people kept buying it, then I had to be at least a little successful. My basic plan was to fake running the store until I really knew how to do it and could make it my own.

That first day when I pushed the wilted funeral wreath aside and put the old skeleton key in the lock, the smell of lemon verbena that always seemed to linger in the store made my throat close up missing Aunt Fiona. At my feet, my cats, Zeke, Yule, Xavier and Winston yowled to be let out of their carriers. (I decided to start at the end of the alphabet and work backward. If I get another one, he's gonna be Vernon.)

All my cats are toms. I'm telling you, ladies, it's a plan I wish we could implement on the other half of our own species. You just take'em to the vet for that one simple little surgery and all their grand ideas go away. You wind up with big lovable couch potatoes who purr just because you walk in the room.

They're all strictly inside cats and they prefer a good air conditioner, which was top on my list of upgrades to make to the facilities as soon as possible. It was early spring and still good and comfortable temperature-wise, but I did not want to listen to the boys complain once summer set in. Aunt Fiona's old swamp cooler wasn't going to work for any of us.

I took the carriers upstairs and blessed Aunt Fiona for her double entry system. The stairs at the back of the store led up to a door that opened on a little vestibule. The next door put you in the apartment proper. Both could be locked so there weren't going to be any unplanned escapes, not that my guys could summon up that much energy anyway.

As soon as I opened the carriers, the gang set out to investigate their new digs. I shut the door behind me and went back down for my suitcase. The boxes could wait until morning. When I looked up at the storefront from the street, there was a pair of cats in each of the big windows animatedly discussing their view of downtown Briar Hollow.

Lots of people might balk at the idea of living above a store on the town's Main Street, but Briar Hollow is a sleepy little burg on the edge of the Blue Ridge. We get our fair share of summer tourists, and even more come leaf season, but it was never going to be enough to have me phoning in noise complaints to the local sheriff's office. That is assuming I'd be able to wake the dispatcher up long enough to take the call.

Aunt Fiona's store -- well, my store now -- is right across the street from the courthouse. My front windows look straight at the Confederate Veteran's monument complete with cannon and cannonballs. We like to tell the Yankees that we're over the War of Northern Aggression because God knows their tourist dollars spend just fine, but truth be told, I'm betting the local Sons of the Confederacy keep that piece of artillery in firing condition.

Next door to my new endeavor on the right, Amity Prescott runs a local craft shop complete with art classes. When I came over for Aunt Fiona's funeral, Amity told me I just *had* to keep the store open on Wednesday nights from now on. "That's when I host the 'Draw Pictures While Drinking Wine' evenings," Amity said. "By the third bottle, they all think they're that Pick-asso feller and they'll buy damned near anything."

On the left, Chase McGregor has his cobbler's shop. He repairs footwear and makes all kinds of custom leather stuff, everything from journal covers to boots for Civil War re-enactors. The smell of new leather always comes wafting out his open front door, and well, to be real honest with you, Chase is not hard on the eyes. And he's a fellow cat lover so we already have something in common. His cat, a lame old ginger named Festus, never limps any farther than the bench by the front door where he spends the mornings taking the sun and greeting passersby.

If the Travel Channel ever bothered to show up in town, they'd label the community something like "bucolic and bohemian." For me, being here is a chance for something more in life than waiting on tables. I love Aunt Fiona even more for thinking enough of me to leave me her shop.

That first night, I settled in her big brass bed with all four of my cats and stared out the window at the moon rising over the courthouse. With the sound of happy purring filling the room and just before sleep claimed me, I remember saying, "Aunt Fiona, if you were a witch, I hope you left me your magic, too."

That might have been where I made my mistake.

ALSO BY JULIETTE HARPER

In the Jinx Hamilton Series:

Witch at Heart

Jinx Hamilton is ready to trade in waitressing for becoming her own boss. The shop she inherits from her eccentric aunt in Briar Hollow, North Carolina seems like the perfect fit. As Jinx handles the enchanted inventory and the unruly clientele, she discovers her aunt also willed her magical powers without an instruction manual!

As if that weren't enough, she's forced to deal with four cats, several homeless ghosts, and a potential serial killer. With a little help from her best friend and a dreamy new neighbor, Jinx must keep the business afloat and the murderer at bay. And it'll take more than clever bookkeeping and spellcasting to keep the store… and herself… from going under.

Witch at Odds

Jinx accepts her new life as a witch and is determined to make a success of both that and her new business. However, she has a great deal to learn. As the story unfolds, Jinx sets out to both study her craft and to get a real direction for her aunt's haphazard approach to inventory. Although Jinx can call on Aunt Fiona's ghost for help, the old lady is far too busy living a jet set afterlife to be worried about her niece's learning curve. That sets Jinx up to make a major mistake and to figure out how to set things right again.

Witch at Last

A lot has changed for Jinx in just a few months. After the mishaps that befell her in *Witch At Odds*, she just wants to enjoy the rest of the summer, but she's not going to be that lucky. As she's poised to tell her friends she's a witch, secrets start popping out all over the place. Between old foes and new locations, Jinx isn't going to get her peaceful summer, but she may just get an entirely different world.

Witch on First

Jinx walks out the front door of her store in Briar Hollow on a Sunday morning only to find her werecat neighbor and boyfriend, Chase McGregor, staring at a dead man. Under the best of circumstances, a corpse complicates things, but Jinx has other problems. Is her trusted mentor lying to her? Have dangerous magical artifacts been placed inside the shop? Join Jinx and Tori as they race to catch a killer and find out what's going on literally under their noses.

Witch on Second

The story opens just a week before Halloween. Jinx and Tori have their hands full helping to organize Briar Hollow's first ever paranormal festival. Beau and the ghosts at the cemetery are eager to help make the event a success, but tensions remain high after the recent killings. Without a mentor to lean on, Jinx must become a stronger, more independent leader. Is she up to the task in the face of ongoing threats? Still mourning the loss of Myrtle and her breakup with Chase, Jinx finds herself confronting new and unexpected foes.

Witch on Third

The books opens on the the last night of Briar Hollow's first annual paranormal festival. With Chase still stinging from the breakup and Lucas Grayson more than a little interested, Jinx has plenty on her plate without a new evil trio in town. As the team works to counter Chesterfield's newest scheme, something happens in the Valley that changes everything for the Hamilton family.

Christmas in the Valley

Join Jinx and company for the first Jinx Hamilton / Shevington novella. In this short read of approximately 75 pages, Jinx, Tori, and the gang head out to spend their first Christmas in the magical Valley of Shevington, a place where anything is possible.

Everything seems perfect, but on Christmas night, Jinx finds herself at the base of the Mother Tree thinking about the one thing she can't have . . . or can she?

The Amulet of Caorunn

Creavit wizard Irenaeus Chesterfield is back, with a bigger, badder plan to go after Jinx and company. In the weeks leading up to Christmas, Jinx starts having dream visions about the mysterious Amulet of Caorunn. Trying to get more details, she and Tori try a dicey double enchantment with shocking results. Join Jinx, Tori, and the gang as they work to recover the Amulet, stop Chesterfield, and enter the mysterious Middle Realm.

To Haunt a Witch

Jinx, Tori, and the gang have settled down to enjoy some "normal" time after their adventure in the Middle Realm. Then Cezar Ionescu walks through the front door of the Witch's Brew asking for a favor. An abandoned house owned by the local Strigoi clan is attracting the attention of the Haunted Briar Hollow web series. Can Jinx and company relocater the spirit?

As usual, there's more to the abandoned house than anyone imagines. When the group brings home a "helpful" spirit, Jinx finds out more about Fae politics than she wanted to know, and discovers a completely hidden element of her already complicated family history.

To Test a Witch

Book 9 transports readers to Fae Londinium. As the Conference of the Realms convenes, Jinx and the gang settle into adjoining rooms at Claridge's determined to find a way to end The Agreement segregating the In Between.

In the three days before the opening ceremony, Lucas assumes the role of tour guide, taking Jinx to Hampton Court and the British Museum. But it's the sites he doesn't show her that prove to be the most critical after an assassination attempt puts Barnaby's life in danger and leaves Jinx in charge of the Shevington delegation.

From encountering the ghosts of Henry VIII's wives to meeting a troop of gargoyle guards in the Fae Houses of Parliament, Jinx and her friends take the town by storm.

To Trick a Witch

In Book 10, *To Trick a Witch*, Jinx answers the age old question, "What did you do over your summer vacation?" Her story beats everyone else's by a mile.

The Conference of the Realms may be over, but the trouble is just getting started for the crew in the lair. There's an outbreak of cryptids in the human realm, threatening witch hysteria in Briar Hollow, and a covert coven reunion in the works.

Jinx finds herself juggling Fae politics while grappling with new career aspirations and relationship complications — all with SpookCon2 looming in October.

To Teach a Witch

The opening of the magical sanctuary of Tír na nÓg has rocked the foundations of Fae society. Isherwood sits in the Tower of Londinium awaiting trial. Jinx and the special ops team circle the globe dealing with *nonconformi* incidents.

Behind every layer of evil lies another bad guy waiting to be unmasked. A crime witnessed by a raven sets in motion a journey into the mists surrounding a hidden island. There, in the company of a king and an order of gallant knights, Jinx will do battle with the woman who started it all.

The Jinx Hamilton / Wrecking Crew Novellas

Moonstone

Think James Bond meets Rocket Raccoon.

Werecat Festus McGregor leads his Recovery of Magical Objects Squad on a mission to retrieve the Moonstone Spoon from the penthouse of eccentric financier and collector Wardlaw Magwilde. Festus has the operation planned to the last detail until a wereparrot and a member of his own team throw a monkey wrench in the works -- but thankfully no actual monkeys.

Join Festus, Rube and the rest of the raccoons in this fun-filled novella replete with hysterical Fae acronyms and overlapping agency jurisdictions. An escapist romp you won't want to put down!

Merstone

A werecat and a raccoon walk into a dragon's lair . . .

Join ROMO agent and werecat Festus McGregor in this second installment of the Jinx Hamilton/Wrecking Crew novellas. Agreeing to an off-the-books mission with wereparrot Jilly Pepperdine, Festus and

Rube find themselves on the Isle of Wight in search of an ancient lodestone with the power to enslave shifters.

Another hysterical visit to the Fae world where magic, artifacts, and laughter abound!

Other Works By Juliette

The Lockwood Legacy

Previously released as a six-book series, *The Lockwood Legacy* returns in three updated and combined editions. The first, *One Silent Bullet*, is available now on Amazon. Edited for clarity and continuity, these re-releases come in advance of the long-awaited continuation of the series in *Four Hearts Bleed.*

One Silent Bullet

A single bullet destroyed a life of lies.

When family patriarch Langston Lockwood allegedly commits suicide, his daughters Kate, Jenny, and Mandy suspect foul play. As the twisted details of their father's life emerge, the girls uncover generations of family secrets that lead them to a mysterious treasure hidden in Baxter's Draw.

Will the Aztec gold lying in their father's private cave bring his girls even greater wealth or will they be the next to die?

The Selby Jensen Paranormal Mysteries

Descendants of the Rose

Selby Jensen's business card reads "Private Investigator," but that seriously downplays her occupation. Let's hear it in her own words:

"You want to know what I do for a living? I rip souls out. Cut heads off. Put silver bullets where silver bullets need putting. You think there aren't any monsters? . . . I have some disturbing news for you. You might want to sit down. Monsters walk among us. I'm looking for one in particular. In the meantime? I'm keeping the rest of them from eating people like you."

Juliette Harper, author of The Jinx Hamilton Novels, creates a cast of characters, most of whom have one thing in common; they don't have a pulse. The dead are doing just fine by Selby, who is determined never to lose someone she loves again, but then a force of love more powerful than her grief changes that plan.

Join Selby Jensen as she and her team track down a shadowy figure tied to a murder at a girls' school. What none of them realize, however, is that in solving this case, they will enter a longer battle against a larger evil.

The Study Club Mysteries

You Can't Get Blood Out of Shag Carpet

Wanda Jean Milton discovers her husband, local exterminator Hilton Milton, dead on her new shag carpet with an Old Hickory carving knife sticking out of his chest.

Beside herself over how she'll remove the stain, and grief-stricken over Hilton's demise, Wanda Jean finds herself the prime suspect. But she is also a member of "the" local Study Club, a bastion of independent Texas feminism 1960s style.

Club President Clara Wyler has no intention of allowing a member to be a murder suspect. Aided by her younger sister and County Clerk, Mae Ella Gormley; Sugar Watson, the proprietress of Sugar's Style and Spray; and Wilma Schneider, Army MASH veteran and local RN, the Club women set out to clear Wanda Jean's name — never guessing the local dirt they'll uncover.

ABOUT THE AUTHOR

Juliette Harper is the pen name used by the writing team of Patricia Pauletti and Rana K. Williamson. As a writer, Juliette's goal is to create strong female characters facing interesting, challenging, painful, and at times comical situations. Refusing to be bound by genre, her primary interest lies in telling good stories.

For more information . . .

www.JulietteHarper.com

author@julietteharper.com

By Juliette Harper

Skye House Publishing, LLC

ISBN: 978-1-943516-43-8

Created with Vellum

Printed in Great Britain
by Amazon

12689096R00142